Come Slowly, Eden

By

Charlene Keel

A Red Sky Presents Book/published by arrangement with the author.

Published by Red Sky Presents
A division of Red Sky Entertainment, Inc.

Come Slowly, Eden

By

Charlene Keel

For all the shy, quiet thoughtful girls
who should reign in the Kingdom of Tallahassee

Where's that sizzling novel?

By SUSAN LYKES
Democrat Staff Writer

A y o u n g woman was in town Friday promoting a b o o k she has written titled "Come Slowly Eden."

It's billed as a "sizzling comtemporary novel." And the writer, Charlene Keel, says it is based on her own experiences and those of other people she used to know in Tallahassee and on the Florida State University campus.

The only trouble is, the book is not on sale in Tallahassee. There is some doubt as to w h e t h e r it ever will be" And if to be told here; those involved don't want to publicize that fact.

The Democrat received a letter from the Dunn, Gadsden, Keller public relations firm in New York City saying Ms. Keel, a 1963 graduate of Leon High School, would be here this week to promote her third book. Instructions were to call Bill DuBey at Tallahassee News if we were interested in an interview.

DuBey, when contacted yesterday, said he had not received any copies of the book in question, he had never been contacted by the publisher of the book, and he was not interested in promoting the book.

DuBey, book distributor for most of the drugstore and grocery store book racks in town as well as for his own book shops, said he considered Ms. Keel's publication a "hot line of books." Not the kind of thing his wanted him to stock their shelves with, even though he admitted there is already a lot of sex on the book stands he supplies.

"We don't order everything a publisher has..... Of that particular title, they didn't send us a single copy," DuBey said.

Peter McCurtin, editor of Nordon Publications which publishes the Leisure Books line, said in a telephone interview Friday his c o m p a n y had shipped copies of "Come S l o w l y Eden" to DuBey on Feb. 14. He didn't remember the number of copies, but said "at least a thousand, I think."

The shipment "went out on the 14th, there was one holiday on the 17th. It should have been there for the past two days," McCurtin said.

Charlene Keel said her book is about two w o m e n at Florida State University, one working her way through school as a prostitute, the other a freshman candidate for homecoming queen born with a silver spoon in her mouth.

Th ey become friends and develop a m u t u a l respect for one another, despite their differences. But tragedy destroys one of the heroines in the end.

The book is set in Tallahassee on the Florida S t a t e University Campus. Real names are used for locations, but all characters are fictional, said Ms. Keel.

A native of Panama City who moved to Tallahassee with her parents as a teenager and graduated from Leon. Ms. Keel describes her in Tallahassee saying "there is nothing worse than almost belonging."

After high school Ms. Keel worked for a year as a secretary at FSU. Then she left Tallahassee to become and airline stewardess for TWA. She now lives in New York City.

She has published a book about the life of a stewardess titled "The Sky's the Limit." That book admittedly exploits the sexy image of airline stewardesses and is "fictionalized a great deal," said Ms. Keel.

Growing up in Tallahassee, and working on the FSU campus, Ms. Keel said she knows for a fact that coeds at the university r e s o r t to prostitution to put themselves through school. "I did meet a woman who was involved," she said.

Ms. Keel said she identified a little with each of the four major characters in her book, but not entirely with any one of them. The characters are composites herself and the other people she knew here.

She said she wrote to book because "If t h e r e is anything wrong with society, it won't go away if we ignore it."

Ms. Keel said her book is "not another Peyton Place where everybody is going to be scandalized." Tallahasseeans should not e x p e c t to recognize themselves or their neighbors in the book's characters .

At the Walden bookstore in Tallahassee, store manager Arden McKenziesaid she had no copies of "Come Slowly Eden" in stock. Nor was the book listed in the forthcoming catalogue she received from Leisure Books.

But it is not unusual for a person to come through town promoting a book one month to six weeks before the shops actually have the p u b l i c a t i o n in stock. she said.

Come slowly, Eden!
Lips unused to Thee
Bashful, sip thy Jasmines
As the fainting Bee,

Reaching late his flower,
Round her chamber hums,
Counts his nectars,
Enters, and is lost in Balms.

—Emily Dickinson

Tallahassee, Florida
Autumn, 1963

Chapter One

The mud made a sucking sound beneath his feet as he cut across the library lawn, threatening to swallow his expensive leather loafers with every step he took. The rain trickled down the back of his skinny neck, flowing in narrow rivulets between his bony shoulder blades. He hunched himself over his load of books and shivered in the premature cold, thinking the sudden cloudburst a harbinger of autumn. He hated his mother all over again because she'd told him to bring an umbrella and he'd refused. Packing and repacking, he'd eliminated many things, and the umbrella was among the first items to go.

It had rained the day he arrived in Florida, and every day since. He tilted his head in a slight angle and surveyed the giant puddle forming in the basin between the sidewalk and the library doors. It looked strangely like a big bowl of consommé salted with raindrops . . . as his mother's tears had salted her soup the day he told her he'd decided there was no God.

She had said nothing, though, so he had asked her, "Are you angry that I don't believe in God anymore?"

"Only at myself," she had informed him, tightlipped, already withdrawing from any possibility of real discourse on the subject. Maybe she had known his announcement was partly for shock effect, but he didn't care. He was coming into his own, as a man instead of a boy, and he could clearly see the shortcomings of the universe, the government, the system, and his mother. His father, dead for many years, was irrelevant.

Still, he wished he'd brought an umbrella.

A girl rushed past him then, the edge of her blue umbrella narrowly missing his eye as it grazed his cheek. She kept on going, not even noticing him—something to which he was all too accustomed. His looks were unremarkable—he was red-haired, freckled, thin, six feet tall and still growing. He was gangly and awkward, and he'd never been with a girl—but that wasn't his fault. Even though he had tried, in his senior year of high school, to ask one or two of them for a date, something inside him, something so indoctrinated into him—again he thought of his mother—left him frozen in terror when confronted with the possibility of an encounter with the opposite sex.

Somewhere deep in his gut, he felt a tight ball of laughter starting to unspool. He sternly checked it. Most of the time he couldn't even bring himself to say the word—sex—with a clear conscience. Not that he had anyone to say it to. He was clumsy, self-conscious, and sensitive; and he was sure he repulsed girls as much as he repulsed himself.

The rain was heavier now, and he quickened his step.

"Well, hurry up . . ."

The voice drifting toward him in the mist was soft and warm and musical. He jerked his head up, realizing as he did that it made him look like a startled turkey, his face bobbing in surprise on the end of a neck that was too long.

"Um . . . oh," he stammered. "Were you talking to me?"

She couldn't be. He would not allow himself to believe she could be. But she was looking directly at him.

"Yes, Tom. I am." The voice coming from beneath the white umbrella was sweet and inviting. An elegant, perfectly manicured hand gripped the sleek, tortoise shell handle. "Now hurry, please. I'm getting soaked."

As he stepped closer, she moved the umbrella aside a little and he recognized her. She was the only freshman candidate for Homecoming Queen, and she was in his English class. Racking up those votes, he thought. But she had an umbrella, and he was already drenched.

"Um . . . thanks," he managed.

She gave the handle to him. "Here, you take this. I think it would be less awkward if you hold it, don't you? Wasn't English the dullest thing?"

"Yeah . . . yes, I guess it was." He didn't really think that. He liked English, and he liked his professor, but he wasn't about to disagree with her. "Hawkins isn't . . . isn't so good."

He'd meant to say the old professor wasn't compelling or engaging or something more entertaining (and maybe even a little sarcastic) than what he'd said, but that's all that came out. She laughed lightly and she seemed sincerely amused, as if he'd reeled off some joke, or some particularly bright comment.

They had to walk close together under her umbrella, and the delicate aroma surrounding her like a halo wafted up to him, snaking gently into his nostrils, mingling with the warmth of her body. She would fit just under his chin, he thought, as a breeze blew her soft, gloriously blond hair against him, making it brush against his shoulder. Beside her, he made lumbering, ungainly moves, trying to match his long paces to her small ones. Her hip collided exquisitely with his thigh. The hairs on his arm prickled, and he grew suddenly warm. A suffocating feeling came over him as he grew hard, and he felt he would choke on his own saliva.

"Oh, excuse me, Tom," she said. "I am so clumsy. What are you going to write your theme about?"

"I'm not sure," he answered dubiously as he moved his books

down to cover his erection. It made him even clumsier, and he stumbled again.

"There isn't a real wide choice," she observed with her delicious, southern drawl. "My Favorite Teacher, My Most Memorable Experience or Why I Like or Dislike College. Variations on the same tired old themes we had in high school."

"Yeah."

He smiled as if he was having a wonderful time, but he felt so stupid. They met a crowd of students coming from the opposite direction, and a sea of umbrellas swelled around them. He almost lost her, but she caught his arm, laughing again as she spoke to another boy as he passed them. Her touch set off such a shock in Tom's body that controlling the expanding manhood between his legs was looking more and more impossible.

She would be great in bed, he thought. Confident, seductive, secure in her own beauty. . . wanting him as he wanted her. He imagined himself protecting her, comforting her—and finally taking her. He would be the god of her body and the god of her intellect, the place where he now believed gods were created.

The rain slacked off as they walked, and he enjoyed even more the smell of her, the warmth of her, and the closeness of their bodies as she matched his pace. She was tiny, but her stride was long and sure, and she didn't seem to be having any trouble keeping up with him.

She broke into his thoughts. "I hate to leave you stranded, Tom, but this is as far as I'm going. It was nice walking with you."

"Uh, yeah. Thank you. I mean—the umbrella. It was a real lifesaver. Ah, maybe sometime . . ."

He felt himself growing red, and he hesitated. His throat dried to a harsh croak, and his voice left him.

"Listen," she said, her delicious southern accent intoxicating him anew. She tossed her blond mane and smiled as she continued, "I really wish I had more time to chat but I'm late now. Maybe sometime after English, we could have a Co-Cola or something, and talk some more, okay?"

A big grin split his thin face and for once, he didn't worry about how it made him look. "Sure—yeah, that would be great." His voice was hoarse with fear but he didn't think she noticed. Maybe she would think it made him sound sexy.

"See you, then," she said.

"Yeah. Okay. See you."

She turned and walked into the malt shop, and Tom turned toward his dorm. He knew there would be no time after English. He didn't know how he knew, he just knew. He was psychic about some things, he really was. The delicious, exotic smell of her was all around him, clinging to him just as his damp clothing did. He hugged his books closer, trying to hide his bursting need—a need he could do only one thing about. But at least now he had her to think about while he did it.

Greg Steinberg turned the page in his psychology textbook, and the letters danced before his eyes like the juggling popcorn and marching ice cream bars in a drive-in movie intermission cartoon. They continued their mocking fox trot in time to the rhythm throbbing from the jukebox. He would much prefer to be in his own apartment, not that he would be any more able to concentrate there, but at least he could smoke. The torrential rain had continued for nearly an hour after he finished at the library, and he pitied those who had to leave the shelter of the malt shop for afternoon classes.

Ye oldey maltey shopey started running through his mind again, joining the letters of the text gyrating on the page before him. He'd never been able to read the sign out front as it was written, *Ye Olde Malte Shoppe.* Whenever he looked up (and he always looked) at the pretentious sixteenth-century lettering flashing neon red and purple over the campus hangout, the sounds that formed in his head and flashed metrically on and off in his mind as he made his way to the same table every day were always ye oldey maltey shopey. In the earliest days of its evolution, it had been the Sweet Shop, and in spite of the colorful neon signage new owners had installed on the last day of December, 1959, it would forever be called.

Sometimes Steinberg ran into one of the women he'd already enjoyed in his bed, on his sofa, or in the backseat of her car. Some were graduate students, as he was; and some were fully tenured professors. But when it came to their nethers, he knew, they were all the same. At least he'd found it so, as long as he'd been comparing nethers.

If there were more than one of his previous, temporary paramours in ye oldey maltey shopey when he was there, he would nod and smile at each of them—but to the one he wanted to have again, immediately, he would give a certain look. By the time he had deposited his books, walked through the line and returned to his table with his tray, his lover du jour would come over to him. He would never have to go to her. And the others had enough class—or perhaps it was pride—to respect his choice of the moment and not try to horn in on the action.

But if he was in the mood to have someone horn in on the action (so to speak), he would phone the second one as soon as he got the first one back to his place. It was a new age and there were a few women—even in a place as backward as the capital of Florida—who were willing to experiment. Even so, there weren't enough of them to keep boredom from setting in.

He wished someone would come in now so the door would open and he could see if it was still raining. As soon as it stopped, he could go to his apartment, put on some Beatles or Bob Dylan, smoke a bowl of the finest herb he could find in the south, and grade the last of the damned freshman test papers. It always amused him that freshmen could be so passionately consumed with an interest in psychology, of all things, when all they should he worried about was getting laid—most of them for the first time.

The door opened then, as if granting his wish, and she walked in, her face and the upper half of her obscured by her efforts to close the white umbrella. Because he was trying to see past her to judge the intensity of the rain, he wasn't really looking at her, not at first. When he did look, he noticed she was having trouble managing the catch of the umbrella and her books at the same time. A burly football hero got up and went to her, offering his assistance, and it was then she captured Steinberg's full attention. That one of these thick-witted gods of the university's socially elite could actually rise from his booth and go to the aid of anyone, even a pretty coed, was all but incomprehensible.

She was pretty. He had to give her that. She walked slowly past him after thanking the football player and graciously refusing whatever he was offering her. Steinberg had to admit she was one he'd like to flat lay into. He'd heard one of his students—a south Georgia farm boy—use the term the year before, and it had stayed with him just as ye oldey maltey shopey had.

"Yes sir," the boy had said languidly as he'd watched a coed bend over to pick up the purse she had dropped. "I'd like to flat lay into that."

It was virile. Steinberg liked to say it—or think it—whenever possible.

The sweet shop was crowded with shelter-seeking students, and the girl with the white umbrella seemed to be looking for someone. Obviously not finding him, she half turned back to the table where the huge quarterback sat with three of his smirking colleagues. Steinberg could see she had no desire for that alternative. What she did have were nice legs and an unbelievably small waistline compared with the firm breasts nature had generously given her. She was standing close to him and he liked the clean, fresh smell of her. He also liked the way her thick blond hair hid a portion of her face as she rearranged the books balanced precariously on her hip and one arm. He reached up and took them from her.

Her lowered eyelids rose sharply, and the gaze she directed at him did a deep dive into his soul. He was unprepared for such a direct, if unspoken, confrontation.

"It's crowded." He said softly, his emotions suddenly, strangely, disconcerted. "You're welcome to join me."

"I'm supposed to be meeting someone," she replied, refusing to relinquish the umbrella. "He's not here yet though."

"I'll be leaving as soon as the rain lets up." Her eyes left him for a moment, and he regained his composure. "Then you can have my table." When she didn't respond, he added, "You might as well be comfortable while you're waiting for your friend."

A smile caught her full lips and parted them slightly.

"Yes, thank you," she murmured and put down the umbrella.

He did not offer to get her order for her. It was simply not his custom. As she went to the counter, he noted the way she held her shoulders back to support the weight of her bosom. She had never been one of those girls, he sensed, who'd slumped through high school with shoulders hunched, disgraced by her femininity.

When she returned, he looked up but did not rise. He noticed the smallness of her hips as she slid easily into the booth, and it moved him profoundly. She glanced shyly at him as she salted her French fries.

"You're Professor Steinberg," she said. "I'm in your class. Introduction to the Human Personality." She laughed at his slow comprehension. "Commonly known as freshman psychology."

He remembered her then. She was freshman candidate for something or other, but he forgot her name as soon as she said it. His mind flew over her polite attempt at conversation and busied itself with speculating on what he wanted to do to her.

Whatever action he took with her would put him in a difficult position though, since fraternization between faculty and students was forbidden. There was no written regulation in his handbook of bylaws, but to openly break with tradition would not be prudent. To be terminated again—in mid-trimester—would be intolerable, not to him so much as to his father.

This was the third graduate school he'd attended in the last two years, at his father's insistence and expense. He already had a master's degree, and a doctorate was not particularly important to him; but as the demand for teachers and social workers had decreased, it was just easier to stay in school with his assistant professorship and the modest allowance his father provided than it was to hassle with the old man. So far, strangely enough, it had kept him out of the draft.

And so far, he had been successful in ignoring the female students he taught, even the ones who appealed to him. Not that he was all that particular about who ended up in his bed, but at least there had to be something there that would intrigue him afterwards, that would make him want to have her again. Whatever that indescribable essence was, this one had it. There was something in her easy, confident manner that inspired that urgent pulling in his groin, stronger now than he'd felt it in a long time. He had no intention of ignoring this one.

She was smiling at him. He wet his lips and asked, "Do you like my class?"

"I don't know," she replied, squeezing some ketchup onto her plate and dipping a sliver of fried potato in it. "It's too early to tell."

He knew her smile was one developed through years of careful training. It was seductive, as her mother's surely was and her mother's mother's before her had been. Those carefully practiced smiles had been cultivated through many generations of southern belles who were born to reign in the Kingdom of Tallahassee. But the knowledge of its expertise did not annul its effect on him.

"You're tryin' to put me on the spot," she continued, reprimanding him in her slow, sweet drawl.

"I didn't mean to. Was it still raining when you came in?"

"Just a drizzle. Do the minds of all psychology professors wander so?"

"No," he patiently returned her smile. "Anyway, I doubt it."

"I hope I'm not interruptin' your work." She glanced away briefly, as she finally took a bite of potato.

"You're not. I don't get much done here . . . but pretending to read buys me a lot of privacy. I was just about to head home." He rose and put his book into his briefcase. "I hope your friend shows up."

She glanced around the room. "Maybe I should call," she said, and looked at the telephone booth. There was a long line of students waiting there. "Guess I'll have to be patient though." Her voice was touched with sadness, but she continued to smile.

"You can use my phone if you like."

"Oh, I don't know . . ." Her gaze took another dive into his own.

"It's not far."

She seemed to consider for a moment. "Well, all right," she said. "If you're sure I wouldn't be imposing."

"I am absolutely sure. Come on. Let's make a run for it."

He handed her the white umbrella and held her gaze in his own. Without another word, she gathered up her books and followed him out into the light autumn rain.

Chapter Two

By the time Tom got back to his dormitory, he was so elated his roommate noticed. For his roommate to notice anything other than a mirror and his own image in it was something of a miracle.

"Hey, man, what happened to you?" asked Jason, slowly rising from the single bed on the opposite side of the room they shared. He actually put down the pornographic magazine he was looking at. "You look blowed away!"

"What?" Tom asked as he placed his books on his night table. Jason was from New York or somewhere up north and Tom could not always understand what he was saying, but not because of the accent. It was almost like a different language. He sometimes had trouble deciding which was slang and which was profanity. He wished Jason wouldn't do it because it always left Tom wondering what he meant, and whether his cool Yankee roommate was laughing at him.

"A chick or acid? It's gotta be one or the other," Jason insisted.

"You know I don't do drugs—especially LSD. That's something I have no desire to play around with," Tom replied, and he tried to say it effectively. The words came out of his mouth with more than a hint of disdain.

"Yeah, yeah, yeah. We've covered that subject." Jason grabbed his magazine again and held it up to Tom. "So—which one?" he taunted in an almost friendly tone. "What about one of these babes? Bet you wouldn't say no to that."

Jason put the book on the bed in front of him. The layout showed a man spread-eagled on a bed with two girls lavishing their attention on him. One had his penis in her mouth and the other was holding her own full breasts close to his face, offering them to him. They were all naked.

Tom wanted to look; he wanted to study the picture in detail, in fact. But he could feel himself blushing, so he turned away. He knew almost everyone on his floor was still trying to decide if he was gay or not, because he was always reluctant to join any conversation about girls. They had no doubt he was straight as far as drugs were concerned, but he knew they wondered about his seeming disinterest in sex. And with girls, as with drugs, it was not really his lack of interest as much as his incredible ignorance about the whole thing.

But he wasn't in the mood to get into a conversation about either subject—especially LSD. It bothered him that Jason kept it right here in their room—little squares of paper placed as casually as aspirin on the desk valet. What if he were to accidentally ingest some of it?

He went into the bathroom and hung his raincoat over the showerhead, noting his reflection in the plastic water-repellant material as the droplets struck the bottom of the tub with a pleasant, muted thrumming sound. No wonder his roommate had commented on his appearance. A smile was playing about the corners of his mouth, and he didn't look quite as bland as he usually did. And the pained, hungry look had left his eyes for the first time since he'd come to the university.

Chapter Three

As usual, Steinberg had some trouble locating his key, and it made him damned glad of her umbrella. As soon as he'd got the door open, he took the umbrella from her, stepping aside so she could enter ahead of him. He shook it, closed it, and crammed it into the overflowing wastebasket just inside the door.

His apartment was cozy and untidy. Books were lying about the living room, most of them open as if he started one before he finished another. There were dishes in the sink, a closet door stood ajar and the battered French doors that separated the bedroom from the living room were bent open on either side at the half-way mark, revealing an unmade bed. He did not seem to be disturbed or embarrassed by this state of affairs. He retrieved the telephone from under the curved arm of the ancient sofa and put it on the coffee table for her.

"Help yourself," he said. "You need the phone book?"

"No, thank you."

"Good. I don't think I have one." He did not smile. "And if I do, I probably wouldn't be able to find it."

While she was on the phone, he went through the French doors to his bureau and got his leather pouch, enjoying the pungent aroma of its contents as he opened it. It was good stuff, grown deep in the woods, in the red clay of southern Georgia, and cured slowly in the privacy of an old tobacco barn. Settling himself on the bed, he sighed and crumbled a fat bud. Catching fragments of her conversation as he rolled, he quickly lined up three neat, tailored joints side by side on the pillow.

"May I speak to Forrest Langdon, please?" Her voice was cheerful, and her accent was delicious, he thought, as it slid sweetly over the ridiculous southern name, reminiscent of magnolia, mint juleps and *Gone With The Wind.* He lit his first smoke of the day and inhaled deeply.

"Do you know when he's expected?"

Silence.

He studied her face. There was tension in her voice, but her face, reared to beautiful, impenetrable camouflage, was impassive.

"Will you please tell him I called? And ask him to call me back at the dorm if he has time." She laughed lightly, so Steinberg could tell she was worried.

"Oh yes, Josh," she went on, her voice becoming all warm honey. "I will be so glad to get out of that place and into the sorority house, for sure. You have no idea how awful it is. None of my friends are in the dorm with me."

There was another pause.

"Now, Josh," she reprimanded huskily. "You know I can't go out with you. Forrest and I—well, you're awfully sweet to ask, just the same. Now, don't you conveniently forget to tell him I called."

Silence.

"Right, it's nothing important. Just—if he's not busy later." She tried to sound carefree, but the smile almost left her face as she replaced the receiver on the hook and then the telephone beside the sofa where it had been before. At once she remembered she was in a man's apartment and a man was watching her; and the smile came swiftly, almost too swiftly, back to her lips. Steinberg was impressed by her self-control.

"Not there," he admonished as he picked up the telephone and put it on the bureau. "I'll never find it again."

She kept smiling her brilliant smile and forcing the light into her eyes. "Well," she said. "Thanks. I won't keep you. You must have lots to do."

"Not really. How about some coffee? It's still raining, you know. You don't want to go back out in the storm."

"Oh, I—" she paused, and lowered her eyelids enough to make her hesitation seem genuine. "Well . . . all right then." She gave in sweetly, her bosom quivering slightly as she took a deep breath. "I guess some coffee would be great, really."

He offered her a smoke from the joint he'd started, but she declined. He did not encourage her. He never tried to persuade people if they were not interested, especially in so small a town where the supply was limited and usually weak—not at all like this precious batch.

For the first time since he'd met her he smiled, and it was genuine. The smile, like the calm that came with the smoke, spread slowly over his features covering them fully, blossoming like a bud photographed in slow motion. He felt a slight pressure behind his eyes, between his temples, and the weight on his brain lifted lightly. The smile was complete, for the calm had taken him. He could now deal with the world and the sad, lovely girl who sat on his sofa.

He put the pot of water on the stove, lit the gas flame and switched on the radio on the shelf above the sink. He turned to face her as The Cascades softly sang, "Listen to the rhythm of the falling rain, telling me what a fool I've been . . ."

"Well, that's a relief," she said. He raised his eyebrows. "You're smiling," she continued. "I thought you didn't like me, or something."

"I do like you." He couldn't remember her name. "I've just got a lot on my mind."

"I guess you have those test papers to grade this weekend. Do you like teaching?"

"Do I like teaching?" he mumbled, seriously contemplating the question. "I don't think about it. Sometimes I do. Like when I run into my students in ye oldey maltey shopey."

She laughed, and her laughter pleased him. It fell around them, smooth and liquid like her hair.

"Do you expect you'll go on teaching after you've finished graduate school?"

"I don't think about that, either. I guess I'll do whatever happens. I mean, I'm not going through life looking for anything to do. I'm mostly in graduate school to please my dad and avoid Viet Nam. Hey," he laughed lightly, almost imperceptibly. "You don't have to make small talk with me. I have no idea what I'm I going to do with my life. I just live. As for politics, I have none. I'm neither for nor against any wars—I just don't think I'd fit into the military."

"What about religion?" she asked.

"Don't have any of that, either. I'm Jewish by birth but presently considering all possibilities, for I am an intellectual—a truth seeker and a man, like as all men."

"Well, then—"

"Of course," he interrupted. "You're too much of a lady to ask about sex, right?"

She laughed again. "Absolutely, sir." She was flirting a little but he didn't hold it against her. It was only natural, considering her heritage.

"Sex . . . ah, sweet, sweet sex." He took another drag on his smoke. "I consider it one of the few natural pleasures left to man, and I fully intend to indulge whenever possible."

"I see," she said, smiling into his eyes.

"I avoid people except when absolutely necessary or entirely unavoidable—or as in your case, extremely gratifying. I like you immensely, but I can't for the life of me remember your name. When I'm high, I have a tendency to talk like a character out of the Poldark books, which my mother read incessantly to me in my childhood."

"My goodness," she exclaimed when he paused for breath. "Sit down, Mr. Steinberg. You must be exhausted. That's the most I've heard you talk since I met you—including your classes. I'll make the coffee."

"Thanks," he said, really meaning it. He liked having women take care of him. "You should call me Greg, except in class of course." He allowed her to propel him gently into a chair. She moved competently about the kitchenette, which was only a unit along one wall of the living room. She never asked where anything was, and when she had made the instant coffee and added milk and sugar to both cups, she placed them on the small table in front of the sofa. He took a sip.

"Perfect," he said.

"Now," she said, after a moment of silence. "I guess I'm not really ready for situations that don't require small talk. It's something new for me." Her voice had a haunting quality beneath her bright, Homecoming Queen tone. "My name is Julie, by the way. I'll expect you to remember it from now on."

"Yes, ma'am."

He felt warm inside, but not from the coffee. He needed to kiss her, and she needed to be kissed. Without a word, he went around the table and drew her into his arms. She did not resist, not even when he led her through the French doors into his bedroom. She did not actively participate as he started to undress her, except moving a little to make his task easier; and she did not resist him when he lowered her to the bed.

Removing his own clothes, he gazed in awe at her perfect body. The creamy, flawless skin, the curve of her hips, the slight indentation where her slender legs met her torso, the perfect triangle of golden hair that matted and tangled between her thighs, and the slight mound of her white belly all worked to compel a sense of reverence within him. Her breasts, uncovered, were even more beautiful than he could have imagined. They were lush and round, perfectly shaped and firmly set beneath a delicate collarbone. The hollow of her throat where he could see her pulse quickening was breathtaking.

He sank beside her and kissed her with a tenderness he did not know he could ever feel, all the while running his broad hands over her shoulders, her back, the smoothness of her buttocks. He caressed the small mound of her belly with his hands, then with his lips. She responded slowly, passively, as if she couldn't think of any reason not to, without making a sound. They moved in complete and graceful silence while he explored every inch of her.

Her passion grew as he used his tongue and his hand to lightly stroke her, and she sighed, her pleasure unmistakeable. Then, when she was ready, he moved on top of her. As he penetrated her sweet warmth, a slight whimper escaped from her throat and she surrendered fully to her need.

The coffee grew cold, and his smoke went out, but they did not notice.

Chapter Four

Tom opened his psychology book and sat with his yellow marker poised over the pages he should be reading. He couldn't study, and he had known when he sat down that he wouldn't be able to concentrate.

At least his roommate had gone out, and Tom was grateful for that. He absolutely could not have tolerated any more questioning, and he had no intention of telling Jason about meeting the beautiful Homecoming Queen candidate and sharing her umbrella. For one thing, he did not want to hear Jason's taunting laughter. For another, he was afraid (he supposed it was leftover superstition from his childhood) that if he told anyone he'd asked her out, and she had seemed to agree, it would not come true.

But it had happened. He had talked to her, and he would talk to her again over a Coke in the malt shop, and then—he would not let his mind go beyond and then, but he grew more restless. He stretched casually, as he'd seen the football players do in high school study hall, fished a dime out of his pocket, and walked slowly down the hall to the pay phone. He knew which dorm she was in and had already memorized the number.

She was not in, and he hesitated about leaving a message. She might not remember him. He should have known she would not be in. A girl like that would almost never sit home at night. He was sure, though, that she had been sincere when she'd invited him to call. He was positive about that.

He decided to take a shower while Jason was out, and he would not have to suffer the annoyance of his roommate straining for a glimpse of his lanky, disrobed figure. It had always bothered him before that Jason and the others were dying to know if he was gay—and if he was, why he was. But after his meeting with the girl, he felt very smug. He chuckled as he undressed and turned on the water. He'd show them. He would show them all. Especially that girl. That beautiful, Homecoming Queen girl. When he got her alone, he would show her a thing or two.

Chapter Five

Later that night, alone in her own bed with her roommate sleeping soundly across the room, Julie wondered what on earth had made her do such a thing. Maybe that was a good sign, because these past few weeks her mind had been too crowded and garbled to wonder about anything. She tried to sleep, but she kept seeing Forrest Langdon's face before her, alternated with the kind face of the teacher, touched with a longing she had never seen in Forrest. Then their individual features got all mixed up and started to blend together—Forrest's brown eyes topped with Steinberg's sandy hair, or the teacher's nose above Forrest's mouth.

If only he would call and talk to her, they could figure out what to do. But from the day she told him she was late, his attitude had changed. A month had gone by with a speed she would not have believed, and it had come to this.

These past two weeks he had not called once. She didn't see him at the malt shop even though she made it a point to stop by when he was usually there. When she called him, he was never in. And he did not return her calls.

She turned over on her stomach and put the pillow over her head. She had seen him from a distance that day after her English class and had tried to catch up to him, but he had disappeared. Then that red-haired boy had almost knocked her over, and she needed all the votes she could get if she was to become the first freshman in FSU's history to be crowned homecoming queen.

She figured rapidly on her fingers for the hundredth time. She was—as near as she could calculate—eight or nine weeks late.

Sighing, she got out of bed and put on her jeans; then she pulled a heavy gray sweater over her head, drawing it down to cover her abdomen. The thought of having to wear those ugly maternity smocks nauseated her and a sudden memory of the smell of the leather upholstery in Steinberg's little sports car made it crucial for her to have air. He had insisted on driving her back to her dorm after they'd made love.

She couldn't sleep and if she kept tossing and turning she would wake Amanda, who would demand an explanation for her insomnia. Amanda was a senior majoring in social work, and she had a disarming way of listening as if she really cared.

And Julie knew if she didn't leave, she just might break down and confide in her roommate, and she didn't want to tell anyone, ever. Not that there was any shame in getting pregnant. She had known a couple of girls in high school who'd had to leave, and there was only a vague disgrace in that. It was the shame in having to face everyone with the fact that Forrest simply did not want her anymore. That she of all people had been used—and then dumped like yesterday's leftovers.

She knew abortions were no longer illegal in Florida—at least not completely. They were supposed to be easy enough to come by, under certain conditions. And even though she was underage, her father certainly knew enough doctors in Tallahassee to make anything possible. The judge was respected and feared by many, and anything Julie had ever asked of him, he had done for her. She imagined this would be no different. If only she could bring herself to tell him.

But she was his perfect, well-mannered darling. She'd graduated high school near the top of her class. She had been head cheerleader, Queen of the May Court, Junior and Senior Class Sweetheart—and she'd held an office in every high school club she'd belonged to. Her genteel mother had spent years and a small fortune making sure she was prepared to take her place in Tallahassee society when she married. She knew she was devastatingly pretty, and as a graduate of her mother's own private finishing school, she was more than adequately equipped for her place in life. And Forrest was perfect for her.

Clearly, she could see their future together—first, the wedding, then moving into the beautiful home her father would give them as a present, seeing Forrest off to work in his father's law firm (after an exotic, passionate breakfast), volunteering her time with some of the social events and organizations her mother thought so important, like Daughters of the Confederacy or the annual May Court Committee. And then, after three years or so, the babies would come.

Then. Not now.

And Forrest was like her soul mate. He was on the football team, so he belonged to the best fraternity on campus. He was also studying law, and she knew her father could open many doors for him that even his own powerful family couldn't budge.

Cautiously, she stepped out into the hall and walked the few steps to the exit. How many times, she wondered, had she let herself out this way to meet Forrest after curfew. Next to the window at the third-floor stairwell was one of the huge, moss-hung oak trees Florida State was famous for, and it was no trouble to crawl from the limb to the trunk and shinny down. Getting back in was almost as easy, for some previous inmate had carved footholds on the window side of the tree, and they had gone undiscovered for years.

She didn't really know where she was going, but instinctively she turned toward Forrest's fraternity house. She still had his pin on her sweater, but it gave her little comfort now. And when she got there, she didn't know what to do. She wanted to go in, demand to see him, and refuse to leave until granted her request. But then his housemother most likely would instigate a full-scale investigation and insist on knowing the details of the early morning visit.

So she waited, trying to draw some comfort from the knowledge that he might be inside studying and maybe even worrying about her. She stood shivering, watching his window for any signs of life.

When she first found out she might be pregnant, she was happy and full of plans. Of course Forrest loved her and would want to marry her at once. What did it matter if she didn't finish college right away, or if she never finished. Nothing mattered so much as marrying Forrest—not even Homecoming Court.

In the beginning, she was full of unspeakable tenderness for the life she carried inside her. She knew both their families would be thrilled when they learned about the baby—after the wonderful white wedding Julie had planned. Then she shared her marvelous secret with Forrest. When he began slipping away, the life inside her became a thing, a cancerous growth since it was so hateful to him. Now she wanted only to be rid of it.

Every thought centered on getting Forrest back. The routes she took to her classes she carefully mapped out, and she planned and rehearsed the calls she made to his fraternity house. The importance of making the Homecoming Court grew into mammoth proportions, for that was to be her dowry to him. If she could do that, she would be a valuable asset to Forrest; and after she got him back, she would be so careful to do everything exactly right, and he would have to love her.

But nothing had worked. A whole month had gone by and there was no change in his attitude. If anything, it was worse because now he wouldn't even talk to her.

She saw the light go out in his window, and her heart jumped into her throat. She waited for half an hour more to see if he would come outside—maybe he'd seen her and would come out and demand to know what she was doing there. Then dejected, feeling like the stupid little fool she had become, she left. She had no idea how long she wandered about the campus with no destination in mind. Finally, she turned back to the dorm. It would soon be daylight, and all she felt was a chill and a dull ache in the pit of her stomach.

Amanda heard Julie slip quietly out of their room, and she wondered what was bothering the girl. Turning restlessly on the narrow lumpy mattress that had served as her bed for three years, she supposed it was merely a case of pre-election jitters.

"I should have such problems," she muttered bitterly; but in spite of herself and in spite of the heavy debutante veneer that covered the pretty blond fluff of a girl, she really liked Julie. They had not had time to talk much in the two months since classes had started, what with the girl's busy social whirl and Amanda's job and various other responsibilities. Amanda knew little about her roommate, and she had her own agenda to worry about.

Knowing she was going to make it—at last—gave her a measure of peace. Only one more year, then she'd work in the field for a while and try to figure out a way—besides what she was doing now—to put herself through graduate school.

When Amanda had discovered who her roommate was, she was curious why Julie would live in the dormitory and not in the mansion her father owned. A person couldn't live and work in Tallahassee all their life without knowing who was who, so Amanda had asked her what the hell she was doing in a dorm. That was the only thing close to a serious discussion the roommates had ever had.

Julie had told her she just didn't want to continue living under her mother's eagle eye, and she wouldn't be allowed to move into her sorority house until she was a sophomore. And since students were assigned rooms in the dorm alphabetically, they had become roommates.

Amanda didn't blame Julie for wanting to get away from her mother. She wondered what her own mother looked like now. She hadn't seen her in over five years and the damage the alcohol was doing back then had already aged the old drunk far beyond her years. Amanda wondered if she was still alive but figured she must be or one of her cousins would have notified her. Not that it mattered. After all that had happened, she doubted she'd feel a thing to learn of her mother's passing.

It wasn't her fault she had been born so late in her mother's life. She was a menopause baby fathered by a dirt farmer who, at seventy-six years old, was practically on his deathbed. She had to laugh as she sat up and rearranged her pillow and her nightgown, which had twisted up beneath her in her efforts to sleep. If he even was her father.

Knowing her mother's preoccupation with the sins of mankind, there was a distinct possibility he wasn't. Anyway, he'd died before she was born, and all he'd left them was the minuscule farm and a decaying produce stand out by the highway.

Amanda grew up at that produce stand. She would never forget the sweltering summers that she'd stood in the hot sun, waiting for tourists to pull over and buy her mother's fresh vegetables and eggs, or have an Orange Crush or Grape Nehi soda out of the pay machine her mother kept. As soon as her mother discovered that people who stopped only to get a cold drink would buy something else out of compassion for the little barefoot, towheaded girl working on spindly legs behind the stand, she made Amanda take over. She taught her how to make change and told her to scream like hell if any man tried to molest her. Then she had left her alone in the vicious heat to read, sell tomatoes, corn and okra, and spray them down with fresh water every hour when they began to wilt.

The summer between her junior and senior years in high school, her mother had taken uncharacteristic pity on her. Often, in the middle of the afternoon, she would tell Amanda she would be happy to watch the stand for a while.

"You go on in and take a shower, honey," she would say. "You need to cool off after standin' out here in the hot sun all day."

Amanda welcomed those breaks, especially since her mother was so budget conscious she wouldn't allow either of them to waste water on daily baths and run up the water bill. It wasn't long before she discovered what was behind her mother's kindness. She was selling peeks at Amanda to any man who would pay the price—a five-dollar bill, a fifth of whiskey or a six-pack of beer.

When she confronted her mother, the ignorant woman had replied, "Oh, hell, Mandy. Ain't no harm in that. Lookin' is okay. They always gonna look. Might as well get something for it. As long as they don't touch. Touchin' is molestin' so as long as they just look and don't touch, ain't no harm in it."

Amanda never worked the produce stand again, and she took a bath whenever she felt like it, after making sure the shades were securely drawn and the cracks in the shower stall were stuffed with toilet paper. Then one rainy afternoon, her mother had attacked her with a butcher knife because she had let a boy carry her books home from school.

Amanda tried to explain that Andy was just a friend, that she was not interested in him like that, any more than he was her. There was nothing between them except friendship, Amanda insisted. Her words only increased her mother's fury. She had first come after Amanda with a leather belt but when it slipped from her grasp and flew across the room, she had grabbed a butcher knife off the kitchen counter.

Amanda had never been afraid of her mother, not even then, not even at her most disgusting and unreasonable. She knew her threats to kill her daughter rather than let her turn into a tramp were as empty as her heart, but the scene had sickened Amanda.

Determined to pull herself out of her mother's way of life, she had moved in with her uncle, paying her way through her last year of high school by minding his four children and cooking and cleaning for his wife. In between washing their clothes in a big wooden barrel until her hands were raw and, more often than not, ironing them dry, she studied. Books had always been her escape and her salvation, and she'd kept a straight-A average all the way through junior high and high school.

Her good grades got her scholarships covering most of the nearly four-thousand-dollar tuition fees for her first year of college, and working part-time in the bookstore gave her a little money to live on. She got a healthy discount on the two thousand dollars needed for her dorm room by washing dishes in the student cafeteria. Still, it was almost impossible to scrape by. But somehow, by working until she was literally too tired to sleep and eating only one meal a day, she made it through her first year. The following summer, she worked two jobs and saved almost every penny for the fall tuition. Early in the spring, she came to the decision that she would not be able to survive at that pace.

Legislature was in session in the state capital, and she thought of an easier way to supplement her income. Before she attempted to launch her new career, though, she researched it thoroughly. She visited both the House and Senate galleries, and she studied her prospective clients carefully.

Next, she went to an underground bookstore and bought as much hardcore pornography as she could afford, ignoring the curious looks the male cashier gave her. Back in her room she studied her purchases carefully, trying to discover what turned men on the most, and what she could do to them that would enable her to charge the maximum with the least amount of effort, or participation.

Her mind made up, she called Andy, her old friend from home

who was also at FSU, in pre-med, studying to become a doctor, and told him she needed a favor. He was stunned when she told him what she wanted.

"Why?" he'd asked. "You want me to take your virginity. Why now, after all the times I tried under the bleachers at Leon High?"

"Easy," she'd told him. "I'm starting a business and it's a liability. I need to get this out of the way and I want you to do it. I'm of age, so you won't get in trouble if that's what you're worried about."

"Heck, no. I wasn't worried about it before. Why should I be now? Anyway, what kind of business?"

"The world's oldest profession. What do you think?"

"I don't believe you. Come on, Mandy—you're not serious."

"Yes, I am. I'm going to get my degree if it kills me and if I keep going the way I'm going now, it just might. There's an easier way, Andy, and I'm going to take it. I've got nothing to lose. My mother thinks I'm a whore anyway, so who cares? And I've got no time for a relationship so I won't be hanging around all the time, like your girlfriend. And don't worry—I would never tell her."

"I don't think she'd believe you. Hell—I'm not sure I believe you."

"Well, it's true. Now are you going to do it or not? Don't make me find some stranger."

"Oh, Mandy . . . I don't know. It doesn't seem right, somehow."

They were in his apartment near the campus. She locked his door and started to undress. "Would it make it easier for you if you paid me?"

"Mandy!" He tried to sound shocked, but she could tell he was getting excited. "Come on, now. Cut it out."

"No, you cut it out. You know you want to." She had her shirt off and was unhooking her bra. He drew in his breath when she let it fall to the floor. "You got five dollars?"

"No, I—"

"It's going to be you, right now, Andy—or it's going to be someone else. You got any money at all?"

He reached into his pocket and drew out three quarters, a nickel and three pennies and held it out to here. "You're worth a hell of a lot more than this."

"That's not the point," she said, taking the coins and putting them in her pocket. Then she unzipped her jeans and stepped out of them, and then her panties. She stood before him, completely naked.

He stared at her, amazed. "Good lord, you're beautiful."

"Thanks."

She unbuttoned his shirt and drew it off, then undid his jeans and pulled them down so she could reach into his briefs. A ragged sigh escaped him and she knew she had won. Carefully holding his manhood, she guided him over to the sofa and finished undressing him.

"Okay," she said. "I don't know what to do, so you've got to show me. And show me everything you know. The rest I'll find in books."

He was only two years older than she and she didn't think he could have that much experience, but he surprised her.

"You want me to make it quick, Mandy?" he asked, his breathing uneven. "I mean, just to get it over with?"

"No, not really," she said. "I want it to last long enough so I'll know whether or not I like it."

And she had liked it. First, they sat on the sofa, where he kissed her sweetly, tenderly. Slowly, little by little, his hands drifted down and gently separated her legs, manipulating her with his fingers as he watched her. She climaxed quickly, but he wasn't finished. As it turned out, he had quite an extensive repertoire.

At last, when he thought he was done, she tried on him some of the things she'd seen in the porn magazines she'd bought, making careful note of his reaction to each. He was happy to oblige.

When she left his place two hours later, she was ready. And she was glad she liked it. That would make it all so much easier. She was looking forward to learning how different men would do it, whether they were all alike, or whether some were better than others.

She had cards bearing her name, the title of 'public relations consultant' and her phone number printed in classic gold on white, and she was careful. She found out where the legislators went to eat and drink, and she spent her hard-earned and carefully hoarded money dining in the best restaurants and making one or two drinks last for hours in the most expensive bars. When a man asked for her phone number, she gave him her card.

When one of them called to inquire about her services, she would explain that she could provide shopping advice if he wanted to buy a gift or send flowers to his wife; that she could advise him on what entertainment there was in the area and she could arrange private parties. She spoke slowly, suggestively, until the caller got the idea. They all, almost without exception, asked what she meant by "private parties."

Her first one had been a little scary, and because she knew better than to try it alone, she'd been able to pull it off. As far as she knew, she had no homosexual leanings; but from the books she had read, she knew there was something about two women making love that drove men wild. And the pictures in the magazines had been explicit.

She answered an advertisement placed in the underground newspaper by a masseuse who specialized in men's and women's home massages. The masseuse became her business partner because she was clean, attractive and willing. She had a steady boyfriend, a sense of humor, and a good doctor that she went to for regular checkups. And she lived in the same dorm as Amanda.

Their first client had wanted only a small gathering with three of his friends and himself, Amanda, and her partner. They had performed well, and the men had gotten their money's worth. Delighted with the service, they promised to call again, and to give Amanda's cards to some of their friends. When she and her partner split their earnings for the evening, she swore, like Scarlett O'Hara, that she would never go hungry again.

Sometimes the fact that she had never been involved with a man bothered her, and she wondered if she might indeed he a lesbian. But she knew that was impossible. When she was entertaining a customer individually, she enjoyed it almost as much as he did—especially since she would imagine her mother's outrage if she ever discovered how her daughter was putting herself through college.

And most of the time she was too busy with her schoolwork and her political interests to miss a one-to-one relationship with a man, even if she had wanted one—which she didn't. She still held on to her part-time job at the bookstore, since she thought when legislature was over, she'd need it. By that time, however, word of her special services had gotten around to some of the leading political figures of Tallahassee, and she was working almost every weekend. As her list of clients grew to include some important city and county officials, she had little fear of being busted.

The bookstore was her haven of sanity in the midst of what was to her a necessary evil. Once she had become accustomed to having enough money to cover her needs, she couldn't bring herself to face the possibility of ever again having to study or go to bed with her insides chewing a hole in her backbone.

Most of the time, she didn't even think of loving or being loved. It was hard to miss something she'd never known. But once in a while it got to her.

Like tonight, when the sheets were warm and fresh against her skin, and she wondered what it would be like to share her thoughts with a man who would cradle her protectively in his arms and listen to what she wanted to say.

She took her nightgown off and got up to move the wastepaper basket to the edge of the door, so the scraping sound would warn her when her roommate came back in.

Turning her top cover all the way back, she enjoyed the feel of the cool sheet against her skin. Lying still, she let her hands glide slowly down her rib cage.

She was still much too thin, even though she could now afford to eat regularly. Although her breasts were small, they were shaped nicely and her clients all seemed to appreciate her slender hips. Slowly, letting her mind contemplate the gentle, handsome, intelligent man she would meet someday, she watched herself move up and down in graceful time to her own touch.

She had just finished and put her nightgown back on when she heard the wastepaper basket moving against the door. She turned over, put the pillow over her head and went to sleep.

Chapter Six

Mr. Steinberg was on Wednesday. The Homecoming finals were scheduled for Friday. She liked Greg Steinberg, maybe even needed him. But right now, with everything else on her mind, she simply couldn't face him. So Julie filled out the pink transfer card, had the registrar's assistant sign it, and put it in the out basket.

She thought about skipping gym class. She was so tired, but lately she was always tired. There would he swimming in the athletic pool today, so maybe it would be worth it.

Her stomach protruded slightly over the top of her bikini, and her body's growing distortion horrified her. She'd always been so proud of her looks—her tight, flat abdomen and slightly curved hips, her naturally blond hair and creamy complexion. She'd never had a tan in her life. She refused to let the sun ruin her skin every summer the way her friends did.

"They'll be sorry," her mother had told her. "When they're thirty years old and shriveled up like prunes, and their husbands start chasing around with every eighteen-year-old they lay eyes on. Don't let that happen to you."

"I won't, I swear," Julie had responded. Her mother's complexion was as creamy and flawless as it was when she was a bride, and as far as Julie knew, her father had never cheated on her. Julie would never give her husband any reason to chase around with someone else. She didn't think Forrest was seeing anyone else. If that was the problem she would certainly have heard about by now. No, she thought. He's just scared. Terrified of being a father and unwilling to be forced into marriage. She could understand that, but they were in this together, and if he loved her . . .

The gym teacher's lecture invaded her thoughts, and resentfully, she tried to focus on what the woman was saying. As soon as the lecture was over, she plunged into the water and swam as hard and fast as she could. The coach had to call out to her twice before she would slow down.

"Carson! You—Julie Carson! Remember your breathing! Slow! Smooth! Now!"

Toward the end of the period, she dragged herself out of the pool and stumbled into the shower room, spent and exhausted. The sauna was practically deserted, so she went back out for her English Lit book.

The coach saw her and issued a warning. "Don't stay in there too long. Fifteen minutes is the limit."

She fell asleep and had no idea what time it was when she came out. She had dreamed about a steamy, darkened beach house with lots of people poking and prodding her, and blood on the sand outside. And then all at once she woke up, and the sauna was deserted and stone cold. Shivering, she dressed hurriedly and gathered up her books. A note on the door caught her eye as she was leaving. It was typed up in all-caps.

CARSON—YOU MUST LEARN RESPONSIBILITY. NOW YOU HAVE MISSED YOUR AFTERNOON CLASSES YOU MUST SUFFER THE CONSEQUENCES.

Julie crumpled up the note and threw it into the wastebasket. Then, deciding to keep it in case her other teachers did not believe whatever excuse she came up with, she retrieved it. Probably pointless, she thought. She wasn't in high school anymore. Most of her professors wouldn't care whether she showed up for class or not. Again, she thought of Greg Steinberg.

Suddenly, out of nowhere, she felt sick. She headed back to the dormitory, and as she walked, the nausea grew. Each step seemed to jar her insides into her throat. She was afraid she wouldn't make it in time. Running up the outer stairs and in through the front door, she only nodded to the girl working the switchboard, and pressing her hand over her mouth, she raced for the elevator. She was grateful it was supper hour, and the building was practically deserted. Her heart pounding and her stomach churning, she ran into her room, threw her books on the bed and dashed into the bathroom. Amanda raced in behind her.

"Hey, wow! What's wrong?"

Amanda held her head and patted her gently on the back as she vomited, spewing out the evil bile that choked her into the toilet.

"You coming down with some exotic new strain of flu or something? Here, let me get you a wet cloth."

Amanda grabbed a hand towel from the shower rack, wet it thoroughly with cold water and mopped Julie's perspiring face with it, bracing her thin body firmly against her roommate's limp one. It was too much, this unexpected kindness.

The tears started and would not stop. When she could finally look at Amanda, the misery inside her forced the words out.

"I—I'm—pregnant."

"Are you sure?"

"I'm sure."

Amanda tried to comfort her. "Okay. All right—don't cry. We'll figure something out."

Steinberg was surprised when the pink card came from the registrar's office that afternoon, informing him Julie Carson had dropped out of his class. She cited the reason as an unforeseen overload and after all, he reasoned, his course was an elective for her.

But she had gotten to him, as no other woman ever had. Her tantalizing, sweet smell, the feel of her, the sadness in her eyes, the essence of her had filtered through his skin and stayed in him, rubbing his bones like sandpaper.

It was never that way for him. When he'd had a woman, he only went back once or twice because he could. The only one who'd held his interest for any length of time—for his entire junior year of undergraduate school—had been a tall, Swedish girl with plain, homely features that were too small for her broad, Nordic face.

But she was highly intelligent and so filled with morbid tastes that she fascinated him for a while. Her curiosity and sexual appetite knew no limits. She was forever inventing new and different ways of copulating and she had an array of sex toys for them to use on each other to heighten their pleasure. Finally, he got tired of it—or of her—he was never quite sure. He just stopped seeing her, and she had never even called to find out why.

But this girl, this Julie—this whipped cream of a southern belle refused to be ejected from his thoughts and he had no idea what to do about it. He remembered how lightly she forced her laughter, how the spark in her eyes would fade, even while being loved, and how she kept forcing it back. She was obviously in love with some football demigod, who obviously couldn't be less interested.

Then why the brief encounter with him, he wondered. A girl like Julie would never be lonely or lacking for affection. She was one of the most sought-after females on campus, the only freshman candidate for something or other. If she never brought this fellow to heel, there would be plenty more for her in the next four years. So why did she let her teacher make love to her? And why did she cling so desperately to him afterwards, as if she'd never been loved in her life.

He warmed at the memory of her body, the pink tips of her round breasts, and the slight ivory mound of her belly. For the first time in his life, he felt a bitter tenderness rising in him.

"Oh hell."

She was pregnant.

He had grown up the only boy in a family of five older sisters and he'd seen all of them in various stages of reproduction. It was a look you couldn't miss.

He felt an unexpected surge of pity for Julie Cream Puff. Then he convinced himself it was just the morning's smoke that was making him feel so compassionate. Again, he turned his attention to the disinterested faces of his freshman class, determined to forget about her.

Amanda knows somebody, Julie thought with disbelief, as she lay quietly on her bed. Amanda knew a med student—someone who could take care of it. Everything was going to be all right. Julie wouldn't have to tell anyone, and when it was done she could get Forrest back. Everything was going to be all right. It was nearly time for lights out when Amanda returned.

"He's out of town," she announced. "But he'll be back on Monday. Don't worry. The main thing is to keep cool so we can think. I stopped at the drug store for some mustard powder. It's an old home remedy, and it probably won't work but it's better than just sitting around feeling helpless."

"What does it do?" Julie asked.

"It's supposed to stimulate your circulation and bring on the flood. Anyway, it can't hurt to weaken your system a little while we're waiting for Andy."

She sighed. Amanda would make the arrangements. She was grateful, though Amanda's competence made her more than a little uncomfortable, which she was finding hard to understand. In this, as in her entire life, someone was there to take care of everything. She had only to lie back, look pretty and let it happen, as she had always done. It was the way things were supposed to be. She wished she had Amanda's strength and perseverance. It couldn't be easy working in that gloomy little bookshop and washing dishes for other students just to make it through another year of school.

It was time for lights out, so they went into the bathroom and lit candles. As Julie got undressed, Amanda filled the tub.

"We'll start you off lukewarm, and then build up the heat gradually so you can take it. The longer you stay in, the better."

At first it was pleasant. The warm water surrounded her tenderly as no man could have done. The slowly increasing temperature relaxed every muscle. Julie's skin began to tingle, and great drops of perspiration ran down her lace and fell from her chin onto her bosom. Amanda mopped her forehead with a washcloth and gave her sips of cold water.

When she cried and begged to get out, Amanda held her shoulders and talked to her of anything and everything. The Homecoming Court. Her parents. The father of her child.

At first Amanda cursed him, but she stopped when Julie objected. "Well, then," Amanda said. "If getting him back is really what you want and you can go to him with a clear head—well, maybe it'll all work out."

"It will. I'm sure of it." Julie settled back, unflinching, into the scalding water. When she could bear it no longer, Amanda helped her out of the tub and into her robe, then wrapped a blanket around her to combat the chill. After a half hour, they tried again. A half hour in and a half hour out, until the mustard was gone. They fell into bed just before morning broke; and Julie slept, for the first time in weeks, an uninterrupted sleep.

She woke with a start, remembering what day it was. She would be named as part of the Homecoming Court. She had to be. That's all there was to it. If she was going to secure a truce with Forrest, she would need every bit of ammunition she could muster in her arsenal. She dressed and did her face quickly, taking special care to get the natural unmade look boys always said they preferred. She brushed her hair until it glistened, noting she would soon need a touchup. She had been lightening her hair slightly since she was thirteen, and no one had ever suspected—not even her mother.

She made it to the fountain in front of Beekman Hall as fast as she could. The dais and microphones were already set up, most of the candidates were milling around nervously in front of the platform, and the band was tuning up. At exactly ten o'clock, the president of the student body approached the podium.

"Ladies and gentlemen, all the votes are in, and I know you're as anxious as I am," he said, taking a sealed envelope from the inside pocket of his blazer. "So I won't waste time with speeches and jokes." He ripped the envelope open and started reeling off names, pausing long enough after each to allow the appropriate amount of applause. "And those are the attendants to our new queen. Ladies, if you'll come up on the platform," he finished as the band played a burlesque interpretation of *A Pretty Girl is Like a Melody.*

Julie wasn't surprised that she'd made it, but she breathed a sigh of relief. As she joined the others, she scanned the faces in the crowd, hoping for a glimpse of Forrest.

"Now from these lovely candidates, two have been selected by you as our queen and her runner-up," the student leader continued, his voice taking on the tone of an announcer at a Miss America Pageant. "And the runner-up, for the first time in the history of the university, is a freshman! Miss Julie Carson!"

There was no surprise in that victory, either, but Julie almost fainted at the sound of her name reverberating around the fountain and across the lawn. If only she could see Forrest.

The other members of the court urged her to take her place beside the ecstatic queen, a tall brunette whose olive complexion stubbornly held on to some of its summer tan. The new monarch tried to thank her subjects, but tears were streaming down her face. Giving way completely to joyful hysteria, she accepted a bouquet of yellow roses and sobbed her gratitude to the audience. Each attendant received a corsage of yellow roses and baby's breath. The student body cheered, and the band charged relentlessly into an instrumental version of *Burning Love,* which Elvis had pushed to the top of the weekly charts.

All the while, Julie stood with a certain easy dignity, staring glassy eyed into the suddenly unfamiliar faces of the crowd.

When the students started to disperse, the girls in the Homecoming Court were instructed to remain behind to pick up their schedules for the busy weeks ahead. They would have wardrobe selections, practice, a skit at the pep rally to write and rehearse, countless parties in their honor, the football game, and the promenade at the dance. And they had to select and name their escorts.

At that moment, Julie caught a glimpse of Forrest walking away, getting lost in the crowd. She wanted to run after him but she resisted the urge. Of course he'd heard her name called with the others, and he had seen her join them on the stage. And now that he knew, she had a legitimate reason to call him later. A sudden surge of power flowed through her. Or maybe she would just wait for him to call her. Now, he would. She was sure of it. He would want to share the spotlight with her throughout Homecoming week. There was no way he could resist that.

The dean of women made a short speech, saying she was honored to be this year's counsel to the queen and her attendants, then she passed out schedules to the court. As Julie got hers, both friends and rivals gathered around to congratulate her. When the crowd started to thin, she felt someone come up behind her and take her hand. Forrest had come back. With a smile, she turned to face him.

But it was Greg Steinberg. Still holding her hand, he drew her gently to him. Her smile froze in place.

"Well done," he said. "Can I buy you a cup of coffee. To mark the occasion?"

"Oh, Mr. Steinberg—what a surprise! Well, I'd love to, but there is just so much I have to do. You understand." She was genuinely surprised to see him, and even more surprised to be glad to see him. And she was astonished that, remembering his touch more vividly than she wished to, she wanted to feel it again.

"Okay," he said. "You're right. Besides, the dean's looking, the corrupt old bag. I'd call you if I knew your number—"

She was able to give him the name of her dorm before another group of jubilant classmates surrounded her. When she looked around again, he was gone.

The rest of the morning went by quickly, filled as it was with festivity. After wavering back and forth, she finally decided not to call Forrest, and she really didn't intend to. But as the day progressed, the possibility of hearing his voice by the simple, easy process of picking up the telephone and dialing a number was too tantalizing to resist. Fear ate away at her newfound confidence as she realized someone else might ask him to escort before she did. He was certainly popular enough.

After staring at her lunch for ten minutes, she went to the telephone in the back of the sweet shop and tried calling him, even though it would mean she would be late for English class.

The housemother answered, reporting that Forrest was out, and Julie knew the housemother would have no reason to lie to her. That gave her enough hope to get through the rest of the day. She wouldn't allow herself wonder where he was or who he was with, because it didn't matter—it really didn't matter anymore. Soon, he would be with her again, and together they would get through whatever had to be done.

It didn't even matter anymore that he didn't want to marry her. Eventually he would, of course; but (she reasoned) why should he interrupt his education and the best time of his life simply because she had been stupid enough to get pregnant. Vaguely, she remembered a brief conversation, early in their relationship, when he'd asked her to get the Pill. She had agreed it was a good idea—and she'd intended to get it—but she couldn't bring herself to ask the family doctor. And she didn't know anyone else.

The sweet shop filled up again as students tried to avoid a sudden thunderstorm. She decided against English. Rain pelted her steadily as she turned away from the campus, and her clothes clung to her ripening figure. She'd forgotten her umbrella.

Miserably she wandered around, trying to shield her books from the dampness, heading for Forrest's frat house and then suddenly changing direction. She didn't know where she was going, but soon found herself standing in front of Greg Steinberg's door. She knocked timidly and was about to turn away, thinking it wasn't such a good idea after all. Besides, he didn't seem to be home.

"Come in!" The muffled roar challenged, as if he didn't really mean it.

She hesitated, not sure if she'd really heard it or imagined it.

"Come in, damn it—or go away!"

Shuddering against the autumn storm, she opened the door and went inside.

He looked up from his book, surprised to see her—shocked, in fact. Neither of them spoke. He simply put his book down and went to her, taking her things from her and placing them carefully on his cluttered coffee table.

Thinking she must look a mess, she pushed her wet hair out of her face, shaking with cold. He disappeared momentarily into the bathroom. He came back with a thick, fluffy towel and wrapped her in it, pulling her close to him, warming her with his body.

When she stopped shaking, he tenderly removed her clothes and using the towel, he dried her all over. As she stood naked in the middle of his living room, he knelt before her. He ran his hands all over her body, and then as she stood above him, he used his mouth to bring her to orgasm. The sensation was so powerful her knees buckled, so he rose to his feet, picked her up and carried her to the bed.

As he undressed, he gazed down at her with a tenderness he had never felt for anyone else. To say it surprised him would be a vast understatement of fact.

Chapter Seven

Amanda had not intended to stop by Beekman Hall after breakfast. Student activities like Homecoming held no interest for her, but it was on the way to her first class. When they called her roommate's name, she felt a sudden, unfamiliar stinging in her eyes. She hadn't cried in years, but she was glad Julie had made it into the court. It was only fair, and for a freshman, the runner-up title was almost as good as winning. That would show the creep who had gotten her pregnant and then didn't want anything more to do with her.

She wondered what Julie's lover was like. If she had to liken the girl's personality to any one object, it would have been an expensive china plate. Well-rounded, shiny and so fragile it would be easily broken if only slightly mishandled. Forrest Langdon, football hero, was sure to be someone on the same social level as Julie and that was too bad. Few of those condescending Princes of the South, Amanda knew, had an ounce of compassion for a girl in trouble.

After lunch, she checked with the dormitory switchboard operator for messages, and the one waiting for her held no surprise. It was time for her gentleman from Tampa. It would mean cutting her psychology class, but she was already three chapters ahead; and Steinberg's lectures were not that great. He was usually stoned and made no effort to hide the fact. They probably had the same connection, she thought as she dressed for her afternoon assignation. She wondered if he also got his supply from Jason.

Assignation. She liked that word. It sounded secretive, mysterious, and date didn't really suit these occasions. She'd never been on a date but she'd had many assignations.

To her surprise, her ancient Volkswagen started with little cajoling and no loss of dignity on her part. As she drove to the Southern Wayfarer Motel, she noted that she had almost three hours until time to go to work at the bookstore. Although traffic was heavy, the drive took no more than ten minutes.

The Wayfarer was tucked discreetly among century-old oak trees at the north base of Monroe Street. It was easily accessible to businessmen and her more exclusive clients who worked in the state capital buildings, and it was safely out of sight in a town that preferred not to see. She had a deal with the manager and always met her clients there.

This would be the most profitable afternoon of the week. The gentleman from Tampa drove to Tallahassee about once a month, even when Legislature was not in session, just to see her. He was in his late fifties, wasn't bad looking, and at least made an attempt at conversation when they were finished. And his preferences didn't bother her.

He had grown up on a farm where cows and hogs were bred, and there was only one kind of intercourse that gave him satisfaction. It was one thing (among many, he'd told Amanda at their first meeting) that his wife simply wouldn't tolerate, which was why he was willing to pay for the pleasure. He'd rather give money to someone nice than go to all the trouble of cheating on his wife with someone who might expect more of him.

It wasn't only that his wife refused to get on all fours for him, he'd explained. He had asked her only once, and then never again because it would have meant doing without entirely for at least six months. She was that uptight. But this younger generation, he often told Amanda with undisguised admiration, had all the right ideas about sex. Nothing is bad, or evil, or filthy or disgusting. Everything is beautiful as long as it feels good and both parties agree. How he envied them their freedom, he confessed.

Amanda didn't mind listening to him. It was part of the job. Besides, he compensated her generously and she never had to remind him to leave the cash on the nightstand.

She always used the same room at the Wayfarer, and she had her own key. After she let herself in and turned down the bed, she set her bottle of tequila on the table next to the bed and stripped down to her bra, panties, garter belt and stockings. Miniskirts and leotards were the rage but her gentleman from Tampa had a special fondness for her pink garter belt adorned with little white rosettes.

Settling herself between the sheets, she smoked a joint and sipped liquor right from the bottle. She didn't use pot or booze unless she had an assignation and she never trusted that the glasses in the room had really been replaced with clean ones. By the time Tampa arrived, she was relaxed and pliable.

"Oh, Mandy . . . you look so hot," he whispered, gazing down at her. It didn't bother her that some of her clients liked to watch her climax, but she refused to let them look into her eyes as she did it. That would be like losing her soul.

Instead, she closed her eyes and made her mind go blank, not picturing his face or her own or the room, just focusing on the feeling of his hand on the most intimate part of her. He wet the fingers of his other hand in his mouth and toyed with her nipples, alternately squeezing and stroking until, at last, she came. She let the afternoon go by without paying too much attention to the time. Then she realized she was going to be late for work if she didn't get a move on. He still didn't want to let her go, so she offered to placate him by letting him watch her take a shower.

He helped her dry off and then looked at his watch. "Sorry, my dear," he said. "Gotta go. I'll leave a little extra for you on the bedside table."

"Thanks," she said, smiling warmly at him. By the time she was dressed, he had gone. She grabbed the sealed envelope he'd left on the nightstand and dashed out the door. It was raining again but she didn't mind. She liked the rain.

The cloudburst lasted most of the evening and she was grateful. It kept the bookstore comfortably deserted so she used the free time to research a paper for her English Lit class. Deeply engrossed in dissecting a verse and noting possibilities of what the imagery meant, she didn't hear the door open.

"Well, what do you think?" The deep voice startled her and she looked up. "Did she or didn't she?"

"What?"

He was tall and his broad shoulders supported an army-green jungle parka. His gaunt, craggy face divulged the slenderness beneath his jacket and his wide grin revealed perfect teeth set off by full, inviting lips and a neatly trimmed black beard. He smelled like fresh rain on pine trees.

"Did old Emily really make it with that preacher, or not?" he asked, his voice touched with natural good humor. She knew he was flirting with her—like a young man who was attracted to a lovely young woman—and she could not imagine why.

"Of course," she replied at last, her voice a little shaky. His eyes were deep set and brown, and they were looking into her own as if probing the depths of her soul.

He took the book of Emily Dickinson's poems from her slight grasp. His hands were warm, in spite of only just coming in from the rain.

"Look," he said seriously. "I don't know who you think you are, but don't blow my one remaining illusion."

"Which is?"

"That Miss Emily remained pure and untouched until her dying day. Unless you're an expert on the reclusive bard."

"Actually," she replied, equally serious. "I am." His light touch made her tremble but he didn't seem to notice. "I've read everything ever written by or about her. At least, everything I've found so far."

"Sorry." He shook his head. "I must cling to my first concept of the chaste Miss Dickinson. I hope you don't mind."

Suddenly she was tired of his banter and more than a little confused by it. There was something in him that drew her out—that made her want something she couldn't even name. Suddenly, she found the whole thing annoying, and she wanted to be left alone.

"You're entitled to your opinion," she said with a shrug. "I really don't care one way or the other. Can I help you with something?"

"Mostly, I just came in to get out of the rain—but there is one thing, I guess. I have a lot of lovingly used textbooks to get rid of. This is my last trimester in captivity. Why don't you come by my place and give me an estimate?"

She laughed, and the sound of her own voice startled her. She couldn't remember the last time she'd laughed.

"Look, I'm sorry," she said slowly, taking her Dickinson away from him. "Maybe you could bring the books in. And I have an awful lot to do here, so if you'll excuse me."

"Okay," he said. "I'll wait. I don't think anyone will be braving this storm, so I'll keep you company until you close up. By then I'll be famished. So as soon as you've punched your clock or signed out or whatever, I'll take you to supper."

"No, but thanks."

"Better not refuse me, my girl," he warned, again disarming her with his smile. "My dissertation is finished, and all I have to do until my orals is follow you around, disputing Dickinson's virginity until I drive off into the sunset with a doctorate under my arm."

She wasn't sure she liked the uneasy way he made her feel, but she let him stay until time to close the store. She knew how plain she was—and still too thin. She could not understand that any stranger who had no knowledge of her occupation—and how good she was at it—could possibly be interested in her. She had many faults but kidding herself was not one of them. She wanted to get back to the safety of her own room in the familiar, comfortable dormitory.

"Okay," she told him. "It's time." She gathered her purse and books and took the bookstore key out of her pocket.

Waiting for her to lock up, he said, "It's not far to the Sweet Shop. I hope you don't mind the walk." He gestured toward the only bicycle now chained to the rack. "My current mode of transportation doesn't accommodate passengers."

"Nice bike," she responded. She thought about taking them both in her car, but she didn't know him that well. Funny, she thought. She could meet a stranger alone in a motel room, but she wouldn't take the chance of letting a potential ax murderer get into her car.

"It's a 1956 Schwinn American," he said, a note of pride in his voice. "Had it for years and it has served me well. I bought it used, mainly because it came with the saddlebags already mounted on the back." Then he took her books and loaded them into the saddlebags, as if it was the most natural thing in the world. It had finally stopped raining and they strolled together in the crisp autumn air, with him pushing his bicycle. Still not comfortable with him, she was glad to see, when they arrived at the restaurant, there were no empty booths.

"Listen, it's awfully nice of you," she said. "But I cut a class today, and I have a lot of reading to catch up on. Thanks anyway." She turned to go but he barred her way, gently taking her arm and drawing her closer to him.

"So let's wait," he said, his voice husky and inviting. As if on cue, three students vacated the booth in front of them. "There—you see," he told her. "It's destiny. Now you hold the table while I get the grub."

As she waited for him, she wondered why she was going along with it. She never allowed a man to direct her, except for pay—and even then there were limitations. All she had to do was get up and walk away. He could not force her to stay if she didn't want to. But more than her anxiety to be anywhere that he was not, was her curiosity at what would happen next. She had never been in a situation with a man where she did not know, in fact did not control, what would happen next.

"You're not one of those vegetarian types, are you?" he asked as he placed a ham sandwich and a bowl of tomato soup in front of her. There was also a large salad with two forks sticking in it and a big plate of fries.

"No," she said.

"You can call me Will," he told her as she started on the soup. "What do I call you?"

"Oh. Amanda. Amanda Carey."

"Okay, Ms. Carey. Now's your chance to convince me."

She laughed again— and it startled her again. "Of what?"

"I love when you do that," he said. "Do it again."

"What?"

"Laugh—and then look surprised, as though you can't believe the sound of your own voice."

"Sometimes I can't," she admitted. "So . . . what am I supposed to be convincing you of? Tell me again."

"Emily and her preacher man. Look here, if you think I'm paying for your supper just to seduce you into a comprising situation, you are sadly mistaken. It's your knowledge of Dickinson that fascinates me. Go ahead. Disillusion me. I dare you."

"All right. I'll give you one example. Just one, because I can't see why you'd care one way or the other and I don't have time for this. I think you're just making fun of me. Besides, if I talk about it too much, I won't be able to write it, and my paper's due in two days." And she quoted softly:

"Come slowly, Eden! Lips unused to thee,
Bashful, sip thy jasmines, as the fainting bee
Reaching late his flower, round her chamber hums,
Counts his nectar, enters, and is lost in balms!"

"Well, maybe . . ." he said slowly when she was finished. "But I still don't buy it. Now hurry and eat your dinner so we can get out of here, and I can seduce you into a compromising situation."

"Are you always like this?" she asked with a smile that seemed too big for her face. "So blunt, I mean."

"No," he teased. "Only in October. The rest of the year I'm something of a dud. But during the Halloween season my charisma is enough to boggle the mind." He smiled back at her and an odd sensation swept over her. She wanted him.

In her life, a few times, she had wanted a man. But never any one man in particular. It was a new feeling for her and she didn't know what to do with it. But she knew one thing. She didn't want to go with him tonight—or any night until she'd had time to remove every trace, no matter how small, of another man ever having been inside her.

He didn't seem to mind waiting and that surprised her. He promised to call her the next day. The rain slackened to a light mist as they walked, side by side back to her car, as close as they could get without touching. Then he kissed her goodnight.

His kiss was different, too. She hardly ever kissed a client. Not many of them wanted to and those who did weren't much good at it. But Will's kiss was slow and long, gentle and sweet, and it reached to the very bottom of her soul. It drew her up and out of her loneliness and showed her what it might be like to be part of something beautiful. A surge of desire shook her small frame as she leaned against him.

"I'll see you tomorrow," he said. He brushed her cheek lightly with his hand and she watched as he unchained his bike, mounted it and walked away. She watched him until he was out of sight.

Chapter Eight

On her way back to the dormitory, Julie decided to try Forrest again. She dialed his number calmly, with little enthusiasm. Mr. Steinberg's lovemaking had drained her, and she was growing sleepy again. It had been an eventful day.

"Hello?"

"May I speak to Forrest Langdon, please?"

"It's me, Julie. How are you?" It didn't sound like him, like she remembered his voice. He sounded so polite, as if she was a stranger. It shocked her into silence for a moment. She had not expected him to answer the phone. She was even more surprised she had not recognized his voice.

"Oh, Forrest," she finally managed. "Hi."

"How've you been?" His tone, so uncharacteristically courteous, set a cool distance between them.

"Fine. Just fine, I guess. Oh," a nervous laugh escaped her, and she hated herself for it. "A little scared because of you-know-what, but that's not why I called."

"Really? Why, then?"

"Well, ah—I just wanted to know—would you like to be my escort at Homecoming?"

"Maybe. Did you get that other thing, that you-know-what thing, taken care of like you said you would?"

"Not yet, Forrest, but I will. I promised, didn't I? I'm working on it." She felt her desperation coming back and for a moment, she despised him for reducing her to this. "Listen. I'm seeing someone soon, a friend of Amanda's, who knows what to do. He's a medical student so you don't have to worry about me. He's very capable."

She wanted him to worry. At least to give her a thought while it was happening—while his child was being cut out of her body.

"Who's Amanda?" He asked. "What house is she in?"

"She's not in a sorority. That is, I've never heard her mention one. She's my roommate at the dorm. Amanda Carey."

He laughed. "You sure can pick 'em," he replied sarcastically. "How much are they charging you—Amanda and her so-called friend?"

"Nothing. He'll do it as a favor to Amanda. She's just trying to help."

"Yeah, right."

"No, really. She is. She's a nice girl, Forrest. Just because she hasn't pledged a sorority doesn't mean she isn't nice. She's trying to help me." She had to raise her voice a little to make sure he heard her over his laughter. He was laughing as if he'd just heard the funniest joke in the world. "I am not going to be choosy about what sorority my—you know—is arranged through."

"Okay, okay. Don't get so worked up. I didn't mean anything by it."

Well, that was a good sign, she thought. He didn't want her to get angry. That could only mean no one else had asked him to be an escort.

"Oh, don't worry," she said sweetly. "I can't stay mad at you anyway. You know how much I—you know how I feel about you."

He ignored that statement. "Just don't get too chummy with this Amanda person," he advised. "Pay her and her friend whatever you have to and let it go at that. You'll be in your sorority house next year anyway so it doesn't matter, right?"

"Right," she said. But it did matter. She liked Amanda considerably more at that moment than she liked Forrest Langdon. "Well, what about it? Do you want to be my escort for Homecoming?"

"Yeah—probably. I'll see if I can work it into my schedule. I'll let you know."

She couldn't believe he was doing this to her, deliberately torturing her. He had to know he was tearing her heart to shreds.

"I don't want to be pushy," she managed. "But you know there's so much to do. We'll need to get together to plan things—wardrobe and practice and everything. I mean, as soon as you've decided."

"When is the first rehearsal?"

"Oh, just a minute." She fumbled in her purse for the schedule. She hadn't even looked at it. "Monday, at four."

"Okay. I'll let you know. And, oh yeah," he paused, and her need for some piece of hope overwhelmed her.

"Yes?" She could hardly breathe. She had to see him, to be with him. To feel safe in his arms again.

"Congratulations."

"Thank you. Well, then . . . I'll see you soon, I guess." Then she laughed—but it was a nervous laugh that sounded hollow and frightened. He didn't seem to notice. As he hung up, she realized her face was burning.

Well, the next move would be his, she resolved. She would wait for him to call her. She couldn't call him again—she just couldn't, after he'd degraded her so. Someone banged on the door of the phone booth. Hastily, she grabbed her purse and notebook and went up to her room.

Amanda wasn't there, and Julie wished she had someone to talk to. Anyone. If she could cry, she thought, she might feel better. But she couldn't cry any more than she could sleep and she was exhausted, mentally as well as physically.

Mr. Steinberg came to mind more than once while she showered and dressed for her date with a basketball jock who was creating a sensation this year. She considered telling the professor the baby was his. If she weren't so far along, maybe she would. But she had no reason to think he would be any more willing to help her than Forrest. Just because Steinberg had gotten what he wanted—twice—that didn't mean he cared what happened to her.

She won, Tom thought. At least, she got runner-up, and that's almost as good. Next year, she'll be homecoming queen, and she wants me to call her.

But of course, he knew she would never go out with him, especially now that she was some sort of campus celebrity. But she had asked him to call and since no one knew about his meeting her, and sharing an umbrella with her, he had nothing to lose. If she refused a date with him, he certainly wouldn't merit discussion with any of her friends. And if she were not there to take his call, then no one would even know he'd called her, no one except himself.

He took a deep breath and dialed the number of her dormitory. His voice, in the light of his new logic, took on an increasingly steady tone as he asked for her. The dispassionate voice of the operator informed him Julie Carson was not in. He wondered if the girl at the switchboard knew his voice by now. He could discern no hint of recognition in her impersonal tone, but even if she did know his voice, it had no face or even a name. And he'd been careful never to leave any messages all the other times he'd called.

He wondered if he ought to forget the whole thing. He would, if she hadn't been so nice to him and seemed so interested. She was interested—there was no denying that. She had even asked him what he intended to write his theme on. Not that she really cared. He'd known immediately it was just an excuse to get him talking about himself. He'd read many advice columns in the women's magazines his mother subscribed to, and that suggestion—to get a man to talk about himself—turned up frequently. So he knew she didn't give a damn what he was going to write his theme on, but at least she wanted him to talk about himself. Oh yes, he reasoned, she was interested.

He started undressing for his shower. If only he could sit down with this girl and really talk to her. This lovely, sweet girl who cared that he talk about himself. What he would tell her. Just everything he'd ever thought about, all his life. And she would listen. She was the kind of girl you could tell those things.

She had looked so beautiful on the platform that morning. So surprised she'd come so close to winning. Of course, that was an honor only a senior could expect, but she'd seemed so genuine, so unpretentious.

He knew she hadn't just been trying to get his vote the day they had shared the umbrella, even though he'd voted for her with all his heart, after he'd resolved not to vote at all. He knew she wanted to see him again.

As he removed his shorts, his roommate opened the door and backed in, bent over a case of beer. Before Tom could grab a towel and cover himself, Jason put the beer down and turned around. His mouth fell open in awe.

"Holy shit," he said reverently, as he sat down on the edge of the bed. He stared, with stunned respect, at Tom's manhood. "Holy shit."

By that time, Tom had managed to get a towel. "Why don't you close your mouth," he suggested to Jason as he wrapped it around himself and tucked it in securely at his waist.

"Oh, man. Don't cover it up," Jason protested. "If I was hung like that, I'd join a nudist colony. Holy shit. And it ain't even standing at half-mast."

Torn blushed, but he was pleased. He untucked the towel and let it slip to the floor. "Guess I'll take my shower," he mumbled with a lopsided grin.

"Does it work as good as it looks?" Jason shouted through the closing door.

"Who knows?" Tom shouted back. The door burst open.

"You're a virgin!" Jason shrieked. "A fucking virgin!"

"Well, that seems to be a contradiction in terms." The humor in Tom's wry observation was lost on Jason.

"With that between your legs? Do you know what a chick would give to—? Oh man, we'll have to do something about this."

"Yeah," Tom said. "I've been trying to do something about it. For a while now." He turned on the shower. "It just doesn't seem to be happening."

"But your dick," Jason said with reverence. "It's . . . it's magnificent. There's just no other word for it. Chicks would be falling all over themselves if they knew."

"Girls don't like me."

"But you like girls—"

Tom grimaced. "Yeah. I do. Look, I know what everybody thinks," he said. "I'm not gay. Not yet, anyway. But I may get desperate enough, someday."

"With what you got?" Jason gripped his roommate by one bony shoulder. "Oh no, friend. You are not going to waste something like that on a guy." He headed for the door. "I'm gonna make a phone call. Tom," he said with quiet determination, "I will personally supervise your deflowering. All you gotta do is put yourself in my competent hands." He chuckled. "In a manner of speaking. Hang loose—but not too loose. You know what I mean?"

Jason left and Tom stepped into the shower. As needles of water beat down with a tingling rhythm on his freckled skin, he laughed out loud.

Chapter Nine

Steinberg awoke late Saturday afternoon, totally disgusted with the world, with life, but mostly with himself. He'd intended to get some studying done that day and some pleasant fornicating done that night. But instead, he'd found himself wandering around the campus, perversely filled with melancholy, and then heading for Beekman Hall instead of going to the library. Then he wasted over two hours in the sweet shop hoping she would come in for breakfast.

Falling asleep during the day always put him in a bad mood. Now the evening was progressing rapidly, and he was standing up the only woman on the faculty who was worth the trouble. Well, he considered, this one was ridiculously plain, although she was a little more than passable in bed and a lot more than willing to get there—and without the social prerequisite of dinner and a drink. He didn't know why he'd decided to stay in alone; it just didn't seem worth the effort to go out. He had smoked some, and thought about smoking some more, but he hadn't gotten around to it. He'd fallen asleep instead, thereby wasting the rest of the day.

He kept thinking maybe Julie would call or drop by, and he was annoyed to still be thinking about her. He let his mind go back idly to the evening before when, with no warning, she had shown up at his apartment. They hadn't even spoken. He'd offered her no coffee or even a smoke, and she hadn't asked for anything. She made no excuses for the visit. Again, she'd offered no resistance when he'd undressed her and again, she'd matched every bit of his passion with her own, making love as if she couldn't get enough of him.

Longing for her again, he closed his eyes, remembering her silken flesh beneath his fingers. Her hips so solid, her breasts so firm and full, her belly so smooth and round and warm with life. He wondered what she would do.

If she got married, she might become one of those martyred women supporting her husband through the rest of college, if he finished at all. If the guy wouldn't marry her, she would have to go through the mess of telling her folks. If her family was anything like his, and he thought it must be, then there would be a tearful confrontation. Jewish mothers didn't have the market cornered on tearful, guilt-assigning scenes. He doubted they even came close to a manipulating southern belle, which no doubt Julie's mother was.

Her parents would release all hell on her, and then they would arrange a quiet, out-of-town abortion, scheduling it so she wouldn't miss too many of the homecoming festivities. They would make sure not a breath of scandal touched her.

Or, if she was too far along, they would send her away to visit some distant relative or to recuperate from some fictitious illness. Mononucleosis was the accepted alibi of the day. When she returned the following year without her child and without hope, her education would be finished. When she discovered her friends had gone on with hardly a thought of leaving her behind, she would never go back. Such a fragile, sheltered beauty could not go through what would be required without it leaving a mark upon her psyche. She would end up organizing campaign activities and charity functions and decorating her father's arm until some acceptable young Tallahassee blueblood could be convinced to marry her.

To hell with it, he thought. He threw down the book he pretended to read and got his raincoat from the closet, just in case. Maybe it wasn't too late to get at that obliging teacher, after all.

Amanda intended to put Will out of her mind. He was not for her and the promise of hope he offered —hope for something she couldn't even name—was just an illusion. Life was too short, and she was too smart to wish for things she could never have. There were no happy endings in her future. She had never believed in romantic fairy tales. It was way too late for them now.

A message from Jason had been waiting for her when she came in the night before, and she still hadn't gotten back to him. He was a good customer, even if he was a bit much to handle sometimes. He was fair about prices, though, and quick to pay up when the evening was over, which was unusual in someone so young. The young ones usually tried to slip out without paying, or they'd try to bargain with her. That was one reason she didn't have many young clients. The other was that she was too expensive for their meager budgets.

But Jason was also one of the best grass connections on campus so he could well afford her. Equally professional, they frequently exchanged commodities—always for the going price. It wasn't easy to find a good connection for smoke and sometimes the weed was all that got her through an evening's work. No, she didn't want to lose Jason. She had to return his call before he found some lovely little sophomore freaky enough to do whatever he wanted to try, and for free. So she would phone him first thing after supper.

Will called at three o'clock.

"Are you ready to give me an estimate on some used books?" he asked cheerfully.

"I don't know," she replied. She had no intention of accepting his invitation.

"When will you know?"

She hesitated a moment, then heard herself say, "As soon as I get there, I guess."

His place wasn't far from the campus, and she decided to walk so she could take advantage of the rare sunshine. In spite of its warmth on her freshly scrubbed face, she could feel a hint of fall in the air. When she reached her destination, she was surprised to find her name scribbled in gigantic red chalk letters on the driveway, and an arrow pointing to the back of the house. She followed the arrow's direction to the base of a stairway. On every other step for three flights up, there was a red chalk arrow.

A note pinned to the screen door and written in red commanded, "Amanda: knock loud in case I'm in the shower." In spite of her resolve to feel nothing for this man, she smiled, her heart giving a small lurch of some inexplicable anticipation as she pounded on the door. It opened almost instantly and Will pulled her inside.

"We'd better not unleash all my beauty upon the world," he said as he leaned over and kissed her on the forehead. Drops of water fell from his face onto hers. As he dashed into the other room, she saw the white flash of his bare behind.

"Be right back," be called over his shoulder. "Make yourself at home."

She looked around at the sparsely furnished room. There was a tattered sofa and chair on one side and a cheap dinette set on the other. In front of the sofa, a beat-up coffee table was piled high with copies of *Time* and *Newsweek.* There was no carpet and no television, but there was an expensive, top of the line stereo in the corner. His bookshelves were bare lumber set on cinder blocks, and they were stuffed to overflowing with books.

Partly to hide her discomfort but more out of curiosity about him, she studied the titles. Most of them were about American Indians and the history of the southwest United States. There were some on education, and over a dozen paperback western novels, all by the same author.

"Not much, is it?" he asked as he entered, clad in faded jeans and a tee-shirt. "But it's all mine—for a few more weeks, anyway."

"It's nice."

"For that lie, you deserve a drink. What would you like?"

"Whatever you have."

"Madame, my bar is not nearly as barren as my house," he said. Frowning reproachfully, he led her into the kitchen and opened the cabinet, revealing a liberal stock of good labels. "I can't afford the bare necessities of life," he went on. "So I see no reason to deprive myself of its pleasures."

"I like your logic," she said, pointing to the tequila. "Straight up, please."

"Lime?"

"No, don't bother. I don't care for it."

"Do you have any?" he asked as he poured her drink.

"What?"

"Logic. You know, basic logic for living."

"If I did, I probably wouldn't be here."

He looked down at her, surprised. "Well, that's a loaded remark if I ever heard one." She could feel herself blushing, and she turned away. "What does it mean?" he asked, gently turning her around and presenting her drink. She took it and sipped.

"Nothing really," she replied. "It's just—I have a lot of studying to do."

"Of course. We all do in these hallowed halls of learning. But you've got to relax sometime."

"Not if I'm going to graduate in January."

"Ah . . . mid-term girl, huh? Not waiting around for the gown fitting and cap toss?"

"Nope. The sooner I'm out of here, the better."

"Well, you are dedicated," he said, filling a highball glass with ice and bourbon. "I'll give you that."

"How would you know?"

"Oh, I've seen you around."

"Really?" She tensed and glanced at his shoes, wondering if he could be a cop. "Doing what?" Not that she really had to worry, considering a top dog on the local police force was one of her steady customers.

"Studying mostly. In the library or the Sweet Shop. Or walking across campus, so intent, on your way somewhere. But I've never seen you with anyone. You don't date?"

"No, I don't."

"Well, you've got to do something besides work and study."

"I've done four years' work in less than three," she told him. "It hasn't been easy, but I'm almost done. At least until I can find a way to pay for graduate school."

"How have you done it so far?"

"Oh, you know. The bookstore. Some part-time jobs when Legislature's in session. Student grants and stipends and the occasional scholarship. But I'm exhausted."

"Must have been hard."

"It has been. So I need to get started on real life, maybe doing only one job. I need a break from the grind before I go for my masters."

He led her back into the living room. "Don't wait too long," he advised. "You may never make it. It's been a struggle for me, too; but if I can do what I want, it was worth it."

"You're getting your doctorate?"

"Yep. But don't let that scare you. It scares me enough for both of us."

"Why?" Another smile pulled at her lips. She was starting to feel more comfortable with him.

"Because when you have a Ph. D after your name, people expect you to know everything, and I sure as hell don't."

"What are you going into?"

"Education," he replied as they settled on the sofa.

"What's your dissertation about?"

His expression brightened. "After I got my master's, I spent a year working out west, in Oklahoma, in one of those government-funded boarding schools Indian kids are shipped to from the reservations." He took a sip of his drink. "Do you know, they get their room and board and a living allowance of two hundred bucks a month from their rich Uncle Sam."

"You say that like it's not a good thing."

"Well, it would be, but Uncle Sam doesn't teach them to save it or invest it or do anything useful with it. The young ones blow it on movies and candy and pop. The older ones blow it on makeup, clothes, booze and drugs. Some of the nation's best-dressed kids are in those schools." He finished his bourbon. "I guess it sounds corny, but I hope to make a difference."

"What happens to them when they graduate?"

"The ones who have conformed have a shot at getting jobs with the school—cleaning or cooking for the girls, maintenance and construction for the boys. The others—the militants, the rebels—their so-called advisors encourage them to take jobs as far away as possible. Most of them go back to the reservation where their prospects are limited. The school doesn't teach them the survival skills they need to make it off the reservation."

"What did they learn from you?" she challenged, her interest growing. "When you were teaching?"

"Plenty. I had a class of eighth graders who could barely read.

When I figured out why, I let them make their own textbooks. See, they could never relate to Alice and Jerry, and Mother and Father and their golden curls and blue eyes, and their dog named Jip that they were never forced by hunger to cook and eat."

"You're kidding. They've really had to do that?"

"They really did. A few years ago when all their sheep froze to death. They didn't have much choice."

"How did their books turn out?"

"Great. They put in all the things they were interested in. Things from home, from the reservation. Things about nature, and of course the sheep." He chuckled. "If you wrote a math problem on the blackboard, they might have trouble figuring it out. But the little mothers can multiply like hell if you give them a problem in sheep."

"What did the school teach them?" she asked.

"Way back when, before I did my stint out there, it was mostly agricultural stuff like shoeing horses, working leather, building houses, and then more recently, things like electrical work and plumbing. And you know—auto repair, welding. The girls—mostly domestic stuff that would help them get jobs as maids or janitorial work. No secretarial skills. A couple of years ago, the powers that be tore down some of the older buildings and built a new dorm and a machine shop. For the construction they used yellow limestone they dug out of a local quarry."

"That sounds progressive," she said.

"Yeah, well. Guess who broke up all those boulders in the rockpile to make construction material?"

"Who?"

"The students. Boys and girls. It's hot, hard work. There's a rumor that some of them died working the rockpile."

"And you think you can make a difference?"

"I hope so."

"It's not corny," she said, echoing his words. "I think you probably can. Anyone who cares so much can make a difference."

He smiled, then went on talking about his students at the Indian school. She listened for almost an hour, entranced by the stories he told. "So, I'm heading out west to pick up where I left off," he finished. "I'm sorry."

"For what?"

"I've been doing all the talking, and I invited you over here so I could get to know you."

"No," she reminded him, avoiding the topic. "You invited me over so you could get an estimate on your books." She gestured towards the shelves. "They ought to bring a pretty good price," she said. "Except those." She indicated the paperback westerns. "I've read a couple of them and they're pretty good. But they won't bring much—"

"Oh, those aren't for sale," he interrupted. "Those are absolutely priceless." He took one out and handed it to her. "They were written by William P. Wilde," he added impressively.

"Well, he's a good writer, if you like pulp fiction, but—"

He stopped her again. "Careful with your critique, madam. I am William P. Wilde, in the flesh. Those masterpieces helped put me through this miserable institution."

"Really? How exciting!" She meant it. "What does the P stand for?"

His laughter was rich and deep. "Prostitute." He leaned over to get her glass and missed seeing her expression change. "I felt I'd sent my talent out awhoring, hack writing like that. How about another drink?"

"Yes, please."

"We'll need some ice."

He rose and took the glasses, then headed for the refrigerator. She followed him. She wanted to tell him she thought it was wonderful to have put himself through school that way. In the hall that led to the, kitchen, he paused and turned to face her. "More of the same?" he asked, holding up her glass.

Their eyes met, and her breath left her body. Carefully, he put their glasses down on the floor and took her in his arms. After he kissed her, long and slow, he whispered, "Let's go to bed. Now."

He took his time with her, touching her as if she were made of spun glass, as if she would break if he did not use the utmost care. His eyes were lit with a tenderness she had never seen and before he moved his hands from her face down her neck to gently cup her breasts, he gazed at her with a longing she recognized, for it was one that had haunted her since she could remember. It was the longing to be loved, to be part of something that mattered, with someone who truly loved her.

She simply lay in his arms, letting him lead the way in every movement. Overcome with this strange new emotion, she forgot all the ways she knew to please a man—and she wanted to please him more than anything she'd ever done in her life.

He finally drew her hand down to touch him, and a slight gasp escaped her. She knew men. She knew every different size and shape and what to do with each one. She was terrified of him, and it was not just because of his size. Unlike any other man she'd been with, he had the power to reach, with his soul, into her most secret place and capture her own.

He kissed her again, letting his long fingers glide sweetly into all the soft recesses of her body. A strange, primitive sound escaped her lips as she thrilled beneath his touch, his kisses, and arched against him with a hunger only he could satisfy. When he knew she was ready, he looked at her face and his gaze locked with hers as he slowly, gently filled up every inch of her.

She sighed softly, and then she gave in, losing herself completely to him.

Chapter Ten

Forrest called Julie on Sunday night.

Her date on Friday, with a football player named Simon, had been a flop, and it wasn't anything he did, really. But he was trying so hard to impress her, not realizing she had already chosen her escort for Homecoming. She had finally asked him to take her home—not back to the dorm, but to her real home. She needed to see her parents. Just see them and be with them for a few hours, to be enclosed safely within the circle of their admiration and approval.

They were delighted, and her mother called the dormitory to let them know she wouldn't be back until Sunday morning. It wasn't as comforting as she had thought it would be. There had never been secrets between Julie and her parents. Her father worshipped her and spoiled her and her mother had carefully nurtured in her all the attributes she would need in a society she had never questioned.

She wanted to tell them about the mess she was in and beg them to fix it for her as they'd always done with anything that had troubled her in the past. The words actually formed on her lips and she opened her mouth to speak them more than once but stopped herself every time. She simply could not bear to disappoint them. She was relieved to get back to the dorm.

Somehow she'd gotten through Sunday afternoon with studying and a Coke break and more studying. Then Sunday night, minutes before lights out, Forrest finally called. She was glad Amanda was in the room. It helped her keep her dignity.

Even though Amanda was quieter than usual, and glanced up every time the telephone rang, her calm presence reassured Julie. She managed to get through five whole minutes of cool but polite conversation until at last Forrest suggested getting together—but it wouldn't be until Monday, the day of the first meeting of the Homecoming Court, at precisely four o'clock.

She understood perfectly and she didn't argue. This dodge-and-dance game was to be played by his rules or not at all. At least he would meet her in front of Beekman Hall so they could go into the meeting together. That was something, she told herself, clinging to a slowly dying hope. Not much, but something.

She replaced the receiver in its cradle and sat staring at it for a moment, hating its ugly plastic face as if it was what had separated them. That was when she remembered to give Amanda all the messages she'd scribbled down that afternoon.

"I declare, Amanda," she said, trying to make her voice bright and cheerful as she teased her roommate. "I didn't know you had so many admirers—especially this guy Jason. He's about to burn the wires up he's so determined to reach you. I think you'd better call him back soon or he's just going to bust wide open. Is he someone special?"

"No," Amanda answered. She seemed preoccupied and Julie hoped she hadn't forgotten about the medical student. She hated to remind her, but she needed to know something definite before she saw Forrest, who would be sure to ask. "No," Amanda repeated, seeming to pull herself out of deep thought. "Jason is just . . . sort of a friend,"

"Well, goodness. It sounds like he wants to be more than that. Anyway, I think it's about time you had some dates, instead of having your nose in those old books all the time. Maybe he wants to ask you for Homecoming."

Amanda laughed. "Somehow, I doubt it," she said.

"Would you—I mean—don't take this the wrong way," Julie said. "But would you like me to fix you up for that weekend?" She wondered why she was offering. She didn't know anyone who was Amanda's type.

"Look—now, don't you take it the wrong way," Amanda replied, still smiling broadly as if Julie had told her a funny joke. "That whole scene is okay for you, but it's not for me. Anyway, I think I might be busy."

"Oh, that's good. Listen, Amanda—" she hesitated.

"Yes?"

"Well, I just hate to be a pest. I really do. But that medical student—do you think he's back in town yet?"

"I'm sorry, Jason. I'm all booked up this week."

Amanda could hardly believe her own words. She never wanted to see any of her customers again, but she had decided to take it day by day. After all, she might never hear from Will again. Thinking about that possibility set off what seemed like an earthquake in her stomach, but she had to face it. Maybe one lazy, loving weekend had been enough for him.

When she had dressed for the third and final time on Sunday, determined to go back to her room and study, he had kissed her lightly.

"See you," was all he'd said. Not when, or where. Just, "See you."

But there was something between them. She could feel it and she knew he felt it, too. As they had grown more accustomed to each other physically, matching rhythm and desire one to the other, her joy increased and she felt complete for the first time in her life. She had never imagined such a feeling. Her orgasms, whether pretended or real, had always been for the exclusive benefit of her clients. They were often self-induced and not one of them had ever been attached to any emotion. She was used to giving men pleasure and taking whatever fell to her by chance, but she had no idea that anything could feel as wonderful as Will's body against hers.

"Aw, come on, Mandy." Jason was relentless. "You could cancel somebody," he insisted. "I'll pay good for it. And it ain't even me,"

Habit forced her to ask, "Do I know, him?"

"I doubt it. He's a freshman. And—are you ready—a virgin! But he's hung like a stud horse, Mandy. And he's so horny he's going apeshit. Girls don't dig him. Hell, he doesn't have the greatest personality in the world and he ain't much to look at, but if they had any idea what he's carrying around under his pants, they wouldn't leave him alone."

"I don't understand," she said, mostly to stall him. "What do you get out of it?"

"That's the best part," he told her with a lewd chuckle. "I get to personally supervise his deflowering."

"You mean you get to watch. Well, you know that would cost double."

"I know, I know. But that's the deal. I get to watch. Every little movement." He laughed again.

"Just watch?" She didn't like to bargain, but she could tell he was speeding, and it was hard to keep up with him. "Because it's not going to be more than that."

"Yeah, yeah. I hear ya. Hey, I'll also throw in a Z of my finest product. What d'ya say?"

"It's tempting, but I can't this week. Won't he keep?"

Just until I see what's going to happen with Will. Just until I get kicked in the belly in the name of love. Then I'll be ready. But not yet.

"Yeah, I guess so." Jason didn't try to hide his disappointment. "But he sure as hell won't keep for long. How about this weekend?"

"Maybe," she said. "Probably. But I don't know yet. Keep in touch, okay?"

It was tempting. Twice the bread, and an ounce of quality smoke besides. Jason always had the best stuff, and whenever they did business, she knew he was good for it. The telephone rang again almost as soon as she hung up.

It was Will. He wanted to see her but be had to go out of town for a few days. Would Friday be all right?

"Yes," she agreed happily, incredulously. He asked if a movie was okay because he couldn't afford anything else.

"I hate movies," she said, managing to control the rising emotion in her voice. "Can't we just stay in and listen to your stereo, or something?"

"I can't wait," he said, pleased with her suggestion. "See you soon."

Chapter Eleven

On Monday morning, Julie chose her outfit carefully and she took extra pains with her hair and makeup. Everything had to be perfect. It all had to work in her favor. Throughout the day, she was happy and excited at one minute, to think that in a few hours she would be with Forrest again, and everything would be like it used to be—like it was supposed to be. So she couldn't understand why, without warning, she would suddenly plunge into depression. In the afternoon, as she walked toward Beekman Hall, she was almost overcome with a sense of dread. She knew there was nothing she could do to dispel the icy wall Forrest had erected between them.

Once, she ducked inside a telephone booth to comb her hair and put on fresh lipstick. Her eyes looked too anxious, she thought as they stared back at her like a stranger's, from her compact mirror. She blinked rapidly, trying to clear them of the deep sadness filling them. Her heart thudded unevenly as she approached the fountain.

He wasn't there.

She checked her watch. She was on time, to the second. A flash of anger shot through her, and if he'd arrived at that moment she would be tempted to spit in his face. She was sick of waiting for Forrest to forgive her for the sin of indulging him, for (although she never really enjoyed it) giving in to him over and over. He certainly didn't take the time to give her pleasure, as Mr. Steinberg had. Before she allowed the teacher to make love to her, she had thought all men were like Forrest. She sank down on the cool concrete edge of the fountain and tried to think. She had to go in, with or without him.

His laughter startled her as he came strolling around the fountain with one of his football comrades. She felt a surprising sting of contempt for him. He was such a coward. He wouldn't even face her alone. With a smile, she rose to full Homecoming Queen stature. Next year, she vowed, she would be queen.

"Hello, Josh," she greeted his friend warmly, offering her hand. Josh took it and squeezed it, giving her an affectionate peck on the cheek. Forrest didn't seem to mind, as he once would have done.

Josh took his leave, and she turned her benevolent, gracious smile on Forrest. "Hi," she said softly, in the old way. "How are you?"

"We'd better go in," he said brusquely.

"Okay," she said brightly. "I was about to give up on you."

"I told you I'd be here," he sounded defensive, and she found that gratifying. Still, she longed for him to take her free hand and put it through the crook of his arm as he'd always done in the past, but he walked on ahead.

"Oh, I knew you wouldn't let me down," she replied, but her voice was shaky and nervous. "You can't blame me for being eager to start the festivities. I was so thrilled to have come so close to winning." He should be saying these things to her. He should be proud of her and excited for her. He should realize how special she was. She wanted to slap him. It was only when she was with Forrest that she didn't feel as special as her parents had always made her believe she was.

"That other thing," he said. "You said you were gettin' something done."

"I am." She smiled cheerfully even as anger churned inside her. "Now don't you worry about a thing. Amanda is taking me to her friend's place tonight. You know—the medical student."

"What's he gonna do?"

"I don't know. He didn't want to go into details over the phone." She came to a stop and faced him squarely. "Forrest, I was hoping you'd come with me tonight. I'm a little nervous. I really wish you could be there."

"No. I got a lot of studying to do if I don't want to be put off the team. You take care of it like you promised."

"Listen—I mean, you don't have to be there, in the same room and everything. You could wait in the car, or at the sweet shop. He doesn't live very far from there. And I could join you after. I just hate to go through it without you." A last plea, she thought. A final petition to him.

"Look, Julie," he said. "I've tried not to hurt you any more than necessary. But you're forcing me to say this."

"What?"

"How do I know it's even mine?"

"Forrest! Of course you know! There wasn't anyone but you!"

"No, I don't. How would I? You were no Miss Purity Pureheart when we did it the first time. We both know that. You better take care of it yourself. I don't want any part of it."

"I can't believe you're doing this—"

"Oh, please," he broke in sarcastically. "For all I know, you could have been puttin' out for everybody in my fraternity. And they'll all say so if you try to start anything. Not even your high and mighty daddy can discredit all of them."

"How could you say such ugly things?"

"I told you I didn't want to hurt you. You brought it on yourself. Okay, look—don't worry. I'm going to get you through Homecoming because I wouldn't see you embarrassed for all the world, without an escort and everything. But you just take care of whatever you have to. Maybe after Homecoming, we can go out once in a while. I don't know. We'll see how it goes."

“All right,” she said quietly.

“Good. Do you want to go in now?”

“Yes, thank you,” she managed politely.

They entered, and her face and her voice carried out the necessary charade. She smiled at everyone, and she answered pleasantly when asked for suggestions. Inside, she was ice.

When the dean of women finally took over the meeting, laying down the laws of decorum to the young ladies and their escorts, Julie’s mind wandered back to that first time with Forrest; and she sank back in silent misery, cursing herself for her stupidity. If only her maidenhood had been intact, maybe he would feel differently. She never should have let him touch her until they were married.

Her mother had been right. Boys would say charming things like, “Virgins have no cash value,” but they no sooner got what they were dying for than they’d pick it up off the backseat of the car or wherever it was they took it and slap you in the face with it.

That’s what she had tried to make her best friends understand on graduation night. For the first time in their lives, the fabulous foursome, as they’d been known in high school, got the keys to the family cars and the privilege of staying out all night, if they wanted. That had been how their parents had chosen to welcome them into the adult world.

They had grown up together and shared everything, even joked sometimes that they shared the same karma since their birthdays were so close together. And between Christmas and graduation, they’d all turned eighteen.

She had tried to make them see that she wasn’t prudish and old-fashioned. But she wasn’t on any crusade to change the world, either. She had a guaranteed position in life, and she didn’t want to compromise it at that early stage. But they’d all had more to drink than any of them were used to, and Billie Jean and the two boys had even smoked marijuana.

After the graduation ceremony and the party that ended at two in the morning, they'd driven to the Gulf Coast because Ronald's dad had rented a cottage for them near Port St. Joe. It was a beautiful, breezy night, with the balmy sea air warding off the oppressive heat of approaching summer.

They parked the car, and then they all sat around on the beach, making out and talking. Billie Jean and Ronald were getting much too hot, and Julie's date started to follow their lead. He had pawed at her with heavy, awkward hands, and she'd protested half-heartedly. She could never remember exactly what happened after that. Only that she had run into the cottage, trying to get away from them.

They had chased her inside, laughing and baying like a pack of hungry, wild dogs. She'd tried to pretend it was a game, even after she knew it wasn't. The boys, in their drugged and beer-sodden stupor, had held her down. And Billie Jean Rhodes, her best friend in high school for three whole years, had undressed her, laughing all the while and telling her it wouldn't hurt a bit, and promising her she would like it.

Then, as Billie Jean and Ronald held her down, Julie's date took his trousers and shorts off. He didn't even take time to remove his shirt, or his socks and shoes. She had cried and begged them to leave her alone, but none of them seemed to hear her.

When her date had finished, he and Billie Jean held her down, urging Ronald to have a turn. Somehow, Julie had managed to pull away from them. The only place to run was out onto the beach again. Thankfully, they hadn't followed her.

She was devastated at losing her virginity so casually, so pointlessly. She found a towel thrown over a beach chair and wrapped herself in it. All she had to do, she thought, as she sank, exhausted, into the waves of darkness enveloping her, was put it all behind her. Put the entire episode out of her mind and never think about it again. And she hadn't. And there hadn't been anyone else, until Forrest.

She had awakened, as dawn was beginning to show in the morning sky, and the towel around her was as red with her virgin blood as the heavens were with the rising sun. She reeked of the foul smell of male excretions and stale beer.

She vomited then, and she didn't even care about so sudden a loss of dignity. What she had left of it anyway. They had robbed her of the only thing she had to bring to the man she would marry.

Having resolved to forget it, she had said nothing about the events of the night before, and neither had Billie Jean. The boys didn't even have the decency to look sheepish or embarrassed. After they had showered and dressed, Billie Jean finally spoke up.

"Look," she said. "It's really no big deal."

"What? That a drunken high school asshole took my virginity? That's no big deal? You knew how I felt about that. You're supposed to be my best friend."

"Come on," Billie Jean insisted. "Virginity in anyone over thirteen is obsolete."

"I hope you're right. I hope the man I marry someday will feel that way."

"Oh, please—It's the sixties. The man you marry someday won't give a rat's ass whether you're a virgin or not."

Well, Forrest did. Or at least, it now seemed to be of primary importance to him. She wondered how many other southern gentlemen had shrugged off their obligations with the justification that the lady in question was no longer a lady.

It was over with Forrest. Oh, he would be her escort, all right. But it was his image he was worried about, not hers. He didn't love her. He never had and he never would. When the meeting was adjourned, she gathered up her books and left him without a word. She didn't look back. He caught up to her at the fountain.

"Hey, where are you going?" he demanded. "Let's grab a bite at the malt shop. We can decide what we're gonna wear for the promenade on the field during half time, and then make a date for the next meeting."

"You mean, let's put in an appearance at the malt shop so you can bask in your own glory," she said calmly. "No thank you, Forrest." She knew how important Homecoming was to him, and for an instant, she triumphed in this small victory. "You can meet me in hell, darlin'. You're only interested in paintin' pretty pictures for the *Tallahassee Democrat,* and the FSU yearbook, and you don't make me feel pretty. Don't you trouble yourself on my account. I'll find another escort somewhere." She flashed her champion's smile at him. "And guess what? I'm not even embarrassed, not one little bit. Have a nice life."

"Wait—wait!" He grabbed her arm as she started to walk away.

"Please, Forrest. Don't make a scene." She gloated as her confidence and self-control returned. "I'm in a hurry. You see . . . I have a date."

"Well, what are you going to do about . . . that other thing?"

"I don't know. But like you said, it's not your problem."

Amanda was waiting for Julie in the Sweet Shoppe, and Julie told her what happened as they walked to the medical student's apartment.

"And the strange thing is," she concluded, "I don't feel anything but relief. I don't miss him and long for him like I did before. Maybe it's because I have so many things on my mind. Once all this is over, it'll probably hit me hard."

"Maybe not. He's such a loser—sorry, but he is."

"No—you're right. He is."

They laughed together, and Julie took comfort in it. "Anyway," Amanda continued. "I'll be there for you, if that means anything."

Julie noticed her roommate was in remarkably good spirits. "It does, Amanda," she said. "It means a lot. I'll never be able to thank you enough."

"You don't have to thank me. Just be glad you got rid of a guy who's nowhere good enough for you. And even if you married him someday, you'd always have this between you. You know, that he acted like such a jerk."

"It seems funny now, to think about marrying Forrest, of all people. And that's all I wanted for so long. And I wanted it so much." Julie shook her head. "I almost wish I could feel something. Anything to keep from being so numb."

In less than an hour, she got her wish. And then she wished only for oblivion.

Dr. Andy Paynter (or at least he would be a doctor someday) was kind and seemed sincere when he said he wanted to help her. But he refused to do anything too extreme, without proper equipment and facilities. He was short and chubby with a thatch of dark curly hair and big brown eyes, reminding Julie of a big, cuddly teddy bear; and she immediately wanted to call him Andy Panda. He smiled his encouragement as he asked her to roll up her sleeve.

"First we'll try the old shot routine," he said. "See, since you haven't done any tests, we can't even be sure you're pregnant. There could be many other reasons for a missed period."

"I've missed two," she said flatly. "And I don't believe in fairy tales—not anymore."

"Well, anyway, if you're not pregnant, or if it's a weak pregnancy, these injections should do the trick."

There would be three of them, he explained—one each day for three days; and about a week after the last one, something should happen if it was going to. "It's not a hundred per cent effective," he told her. "But there's only one other thing I know to do and I'd like to give the shots a chance first." And he absolutely refused her offer of money. He had managed to cop the drug from the hospital pharmacy where he worked part-time, he explained. Anyway, he said, any friend of Amanda's was a friend of his.

Andy offered a long discourse in favor of making abortions available to minors without question, and without informing their parents. She listened politely until the drug started to take effect. At first she felt dizzy, and then her throat and mouth turned to cotton, and she had trouble breathing. She stood up and tried to walk, only to find that her legs seemed to be miles away from her body.

"Here," he suggested kindly. "You'd better go in and lie down." He helped her into the bedroom. "It won't last long—not more than an hour or so. Don't get scared. It's sort of like a bad acid trip. Just lie still and try to think about good things in the future," he comforted her as he put a light blanket over her. Later, she would remember thinking what a good doctor he was going to be, with that marvelous bedside manner.

It seemed she heard his voice and Amanda's coming over a great distance, even though they were in the next room, and she thought she was going to black out. She felt pain, but she didn't know where, and she was afraid she was going to be sick. She had never felt so nauseated, not even in those mornings when she had first feared she was pregnant. But nothing happened. Gradually it stopped. It lasted no longer than he said it would. When her head cleared, she sat up and found she was incredibly sleepy.

She would get through the other two injections somehow. But the only thing she wanted now was sleep. Lovely, uncomplicated, undemanding sleep.

"I won't be long, Andy," she heard Amanda say as she was putting on her sweater. "I want to make sure she gets back to the dorm okay. I'm famished too. I'll meet you at the Sweet Shoppe. It'll be my treat."

Gratefully, Julie leaned against Amanda's strong, slender form, allowing her roommate to guide her back to the dormitory and put her to bed. She didn't even mind that Amanda was going out again. She felt safe. Everything was going to be all right.

Chapter Twelve

"Just one moment, I'll connect you."

Tom leaned on the door of the telephone booth as he waited, completely relaxed. The chemistry test and the three hours of studying he'd put in at the library had drained him. He didn't expect to ever see her again anyway, except in English class, where she never seemed to see him. But it was a large class of freshmen, most of them trying to impress the inexperienced professor who wasn't much older than his students, all of them eager to get English 101 out of the way. Tom was calling Julie more out of habit than hope and when be heard her voice at the end of the line, his surprise left him speechless.

"Hello?" When he didn't say anything, she asked, "Who is this?"

"Hi, Julie," he managed. His voice cracked, but he recovered right away. "It's Tom, from English. I mean, we have English together. One day we shared an umbrella, remember?"

"Oh, of course. How are you, Tom?"

He breathed a sigh of relief and went on quickly, afraid she had heard the sigh, "Um, how did you do with your theme?" Oh crap, he thought. That sounded so stupid. He'd heard Jason on the phone with various girls, and they never seemed to be talking about school.

"Not very well, I'm afraid. You know, so much has been happening—"

"Oh, right." He was irrevocably dense. "I forgot to congratulate you. You know—on making the homecoming court. Congratulations."

"Why, thank you, Tom." Dear God, she sounded so sweet. There was silence as she waited for him to speak. He had to say something. After a moment she went on, "How did you do?"

He'd lost all sense of time and place and had no idea what she meant.

"With your theme?" she prompted.

"Oh . . . ah, okay, I guess." He cringed at his own social incompetence but decided to plunge headlong into what he wanted to say before he lost his nerve completely. "But . . . uh . . . that isn't what I called about."

There was a long pause, when it seemed like his tongue was stuck in concrete, before she prompted. "It's not?" she said, her voice so sweet it made him light-headed. "Well, what did you call about?"

"I was wondering if maybe you might want to . . . I mean . . . would you like to have a Coke after English tomorrow?" He blurted it all out in one breath. It was the only way he could get it out at all.

"Tom, I would just love to, sometime. But right now, what with all the demands of homecoming. Well, you understand, I know. My time is so limited at the moment."

"Sure. Right. Maybe after homecoming?"

"That sounds really nice."

He said something like, "Okay, then. See you in English," and he hung up. He was disappointed, of course, but not like he would have been if she had simply refused him. All he had to do was wait until this stupid homecoming nonsense was over with. Then they would have all year, and next year, and two more years after that, to be together. For surely, they would be together. It would happen. He would have her, and she would love it. He knew it, and he was content to wait.

When he got back to his room, Jason was dressing to go out.

"Want to go?" he asked Tom.

"Where?" Tom asked hopefully, his loins coming painfully to life.

"Friend of mine. He's a sophomore and he lives off campus. He just got some dynamite shit from his chick in Boston."

"Oh, you mean drugs. No thanks. Hey, did you ever get in touch with that girl?"

"I certainly did, and she's gonna try to keep the weekend open for us. Don't worry—you're as good as ruined. Come on, man—come with. You could use a good smoke more than me."

Tom knew that Jason sometimes did not get back until morning. "I really don't think so. But thanks anyway."

"Okay, but you know it's just a matter of time," he rolled his eyes insanely. "I will draw you into the dark side of life and use your power well." Playfully, he punched Tom's shoulder. "Hell, you got enough down there to attract an unending stream of women for both of us."

Tom laughed as his roommate sidled out the door with the deranged expression still on his face. Although he was curious as to what went on at these get-togethers Jason invited him to, he had more important things to think about. Still, he found Jason's determination to include him immensely flattering.

He was infinitely pleased with himself. Something had opened in him and he was better able to communicate with people, to open up to them. It had taken only a few weeks away from his mother, and he was becoming a different person. He owed her a letter, but he resolved not to write to her for at least a week.

It was only after she hung up the phone that Julie realized who had been on the other end of the line. The red-haired boy who had looked so pathetic that day, with the rain flattening his thin, wispy hair to his skinny head. Red-haired, freckled, emaciated, and absolutely lacking as far as looks went. She had felt sorry for him—and she needed his vote—so she'd invited him to share her umbrella.

For one bitter moment, she considered asking him to escort her for homecoming weekend. That would show Forrest—it would show them all. All the Right People who had always been with her at the forefront of every dance, every beauty or poise or popularity contest, every tea or banquet. The Right People who were with her in all the Right Places to be, who'd somehow shaped her life into this ugly mess. Having someone like Tom as her escort would show them all, but it was impossible.

She couldn't do that to herself, and she wouldn't be able to tolerate him for one evening, let alone throughout the entire weekend. And she might as well have as much fun as possible under the circumstances.

Returning to her preparations for the next day, she checked the skirt and blouse she planned to wear and then she set her hair and creamed her face. When she turned to her bed—ravaged and topsy turvy—she couldn't help comparing it with Amanda's, which was neatly made, corners tucked in and not a wrinkle anywhere. Julie wished her roommate was in, but she hadn't come back from supper with the cuddly, young almost doctor.

Andy was the first guy to take an interest in Amanda since the beginning of school, except for the mysterious Jason. Until Julie had been dormitory-bound waiting for Forrest to call, she'd never noticed how many calls Amanda got—but even so, she never seemed to have any dates, or to talk about them if she did. As Julie climbed into bed, she thought Andy would be perfect for Amanda. Social workers and doctors would probably have a lot to talk about.

She couldn't sleep, so she got up and looked for something to read. It was infuriating. During the day, she could barely keep her head off her desk and her eyes open. At night, she couldn't close them, and even if she could it was impossible to find a comfortable position. She was used to sleeping on her stomach, but the Thing, as she'd come to think of it, was now a hard knot above her pubic bone, just large enough to pinch if she dared to offend it with her weight.

She wondered vaguely, why she worried so about hurting it herself. Putting herself in the hands of Amanda and her doctor friend seemed to remove Julie somehow, to make her no more than an interested bystander. Was it possible, she wondered, to have any maternal instincts toward a baby she wasn't even going to keep? That bothered her a little—enough to make sleep impossible.

It was getting too cold to go out through the window, and she really didn't feel up to it after her ordeal that day. With the realization that she no longer wanted Forrest Langdon in her life, came the loss of all desire to go wandering around the campus at night. As much as she had loved Forrest—or thought she loved him—she now hated him. Whenever his mocking face flashed through her brain, she closed her eyes and willed it away. If she were a man, or if she had brothers to do it, she would see him beaten senseless. She wished she could cry but somehow no tears would come.

Twice more she would have those awful injections, and afterwards, more waiting to see if it would work. It was what she wanted, she told herself. She couldn't have a baby—not now. She wouldn't know how to take care of a baby, for heaven's sake. And she couldn't do that to her parents. They had such wonderful plans for her.

No, she couldn't do that to them, or to herself, so she would see it through. She would take the shots, expel the Thing and get on with her life. But somehow, the thought that it was almost over gave her no comfort at all. She had started to wonder what the Thing would look like, and she had dreamed she was holding it. Sometimes she could almost feel it in her arms.

She slept so deeply that the next morning her roommate had to pull the covers off her and shake her awake.

"Hey, get up. You're gonna be late," Amanda commanded, as she grabbed her sweater and shouldered her burden of books, "And don't forget to meet me this afternoon."

"Like I would," Julie mumbled, struggling for wakefulness.

The second and last injections were as terrible as the first. But with Amanda and Andy talking quietly in the next room, Julie wrestled with the nausea and the drug's assault on her body until at last she felt able to walk back to the dormitory. She was grateful that the weird, sickish sensation didn't last long—just long enough to make her think she would vomit her insides clear over the edge of eternity. And then it would abruptly stop at the brink and her mind and body could turn around and drift back down into reality.

About a week, Andy told her, before she could expect to finally get her period. That was an odd way of putting it, she thought—getting something good as opposed to expelling something unwanted. Maybe the waiting wouldn't be so hard because she had all the homecoming business to fill her time, but she was confident it would happen, and then all would be well.

But now, inexplicably, the thought filled her with an infinite sadness, which she tried to ward off by throwing herself into the festivities with renewed energy. She accepted every date she could manage, gloating over the fact that every egotistical male in her circle of friends who had not yet been asked to escort was blatantly wooing her. To her delight, word had quickly spread across campus that the runner-up had dumped her boyfriend and had not chosen anyone.

At the last possible minute, in a burst of contempt for every member of what she had begun to consider an alien sex, she decided to ask her cousin. He was a few years older than she, and they had always enjoyed a right-back-at-you, teasing kind of relationship. He was a graduate student, and though he always made the dean's list, he had never had the honor—or the inclination, as far as she knew—of actively participating in homecoming.

It would mean he'd have to wear a suit and tie and get a haircut, but she knew he would not refuse her. If only she could get him to shave off the beard. Maybe together, she and her mother could persuade him.

Chapter Thirteen

With an aching, ancient sweetness, Amanda yielded at last to the feeling gradually, insistently consuming her. Having no preconception or experience of love on any personal level, it was an absorbing and bewildering emotion. The moment she let herself think of Will's mouth on hers or allowed herself to dwell on the tender expression in his eyes whenever he looked at her, she would literally forget to breathe.

When he looked at her. When he looked at her, he somehow saw who she was, at her core, as she was meant to be—and not what she had become. Even that was a small miracle. It was at odds with everything she knew about herself, but she was almost ready to believe he really, truly liked her and that he knew nothing more about her than what she had chosen to tell him, which so far wasn't much.

Whenever the conversation turned toward herself, she always managed to change the subject. She'd told him only that she was estranged from her mother and was putting herself through school by working in the bookstore and qualifying for student grants, and that she intended to go into some branch of social work. When they had talked, she made sure to turn the conversation back on him.

When they talked. Another miracle.

Again, she had to fight the strange, suffocating pressure that overwhelmed her when she couldn't control her thoughts, when—

usually in the gray twilight of morning—he would come crashing into her mind.

When they had talked, it was about everything, and about nothing. But they had communicated. They had understood each other, had anticipated each other's words and finished each other's sentences. And sometimes, there was no need to complete a sentence; and their words had ended with sweet, tender kisses.

She pushed her drowsy reverie into the far recesses of her consciousness before it could lead her softly back to sleep. She barely had time for a shower before her first class. It would be a good day. Fridays were easy—only three classes and a short, two-hour stint in the bookstore. And then—tonight—she would be with Will again.

A heavy lump of doubt settled in the pit of her stomach, and she knew breakfast would be impossible. He had not called during the week, and the fear she would never see him again threatened to overcast the entire day. Despite her efforts to shake it off, it clung to her. The doubt seemed not to stem from faith, or trust, or even logic. It seemed to have an obsessive mind of its own—a second, ugly personality—and it delighted in torturing her.

She felt a little guilty for being glad Julie's misfortune had kept her busy during the week. She was never happy about other people's problems, but if she hadn't taken it upon herself to help her roommate, she would have gone out of her mind, thinking about Will.

"Everything's going to work out fine," she'd told Julie and she had repeated the assurance as needed. Because she knew—but didn't say—things always worked out for beautiful, lighthearted girls like Julie.

Amanda didn't really have much faith in the injections, but it was better than doing nothing. And when every other practical resource was exhausted, Julie's loving parents would make sure she got the best of care. They would fly her first class to New York or some other glamorous, distant city where no one would ever find out about her problem, and they would put her in a luxurious hotel to recover from an abortion by one of the country's best doctors. After her ordeal, she would do some shopping and come back to Tallahassee with a new spring wardrobe.

And Amanda was equally grateful that this time Andy accepted her barter deal—a good dinner at a great restaurant—for each shot. Andy had grown up as a foster child on a farm down the road from her mother's vegetable stand. He was kind because the people who raised him were kind to him and although they never officially adopted him, they were supporting him through college. She had paid Andy for medical services only once with sex, not long after that first time when she'd insisted he take her virginity, but that was before she was making enough of a profit to pay him in cash.

By the time she got to the bookstore, she had such a headache she thought her brain would explode. Every hour, she checked with the switchboard at the dorm, but there was no message from Will. So, she thought, that was it. He wasn't going to call. It was over and she'd better damn well accept it. She gave up trying to study and with patient resignation, she assisted the few customers who came into the shop.

Fifteen minutes before time for her to lock up, Will sauntered in. He was grinning broadly.

"Well, my sad-eyed lady," he greeted her cheerfully. "Ready to go to my den of iniquity and lie with me?"

"Oh, I . . . yes, I am," she stammered as relief overwhelmed her. "I thought you weren't coming."

"Shame on you. I said I'd be here, didn't I?"

"Right," she said and smiled. Then she turned away to hide the tears that started in spite of her resolve.

They went to his apartment, and he made scrambled eggs and toast for dinner. They drank coffee and talked about the week; then he took her cup away from her and pulled her down on the sofa beside him.

He sat with her there for a while with one arm around her, letting her head rest on his shoulder as his cheek brushed her hair. When they moved into his bedroom at last, he undressed her, gently caressing her flesh as each bit of it was exposed. It seemed he savored these moments together just as she did.

He made her lie down on the bed and he ran his hands slowly over her body, looking at her in awe, as if she were some apparition that might disappear before his eyes. When at last he entered her, it was with a grace and a strength that made her wonder. Who was she, to inspire such tenderness in someone as truly magnificent a person as he was?

She tried to convince herself that the first time they made love, her sense of fulfillment, of completion, had been a joyous accident, some cynical joke nature had played on her, and it most assuredly could not happen again. But it did. And each time he made it happen for her, it tore her soul to pieces, for she knew it would end. Everything ended sooner or later. The only trouble was that it had never mattered before.

At first, she slept restlessly in his arms, waking often to touch him, to press against him, to reassure herself that she was really there beside him. On Saturday they ate little, studied hardly at all, and made love endlessly. Saturday night, she tried not to sleep because she wanted to etch it all into her mind—the feel and smell and taste of him—to store up the memory of every moment against a bleak future without him. She lay in his arms, her fingers curled in his hair, as she watched him sleep. He stirred once or twice and hugged her closer. When a tear trickled from her eyes onto his shoulder, he kissed her forehead, and was lost again in sleep.

By Sunday, she wondered how she could ever survive without him but of course she would find a way when the time came. The awful life she had endured and escaped before she'd met Will had been nothing but poverty and disappointment. Disappointment was nothing new to her, but she could not bear to think of life without Will.

They made love again that afternoon, both of them stunned anew at their absolute physical compatibility. The ringing of the telephone pierced the velvet silence surrounding them as they lay together on his bed, limbs entwined, still warm from their mutual passion.

"I'm not answering that," he declared softly.

"It might be important," she offered, and hated herself the instant she said it.

"Well, if you insist," he said and got up, not bothering to cover himself. She was glad. She enjoyed the long, lean look of him as he padded out to the living room. "Hello," he said into the receiver, his tone clearly meant to discourage conversation. Then, "Oh hi, love. How've you been?"

He paused and Amanda's heart turned merciless cartwheels across her lungs. She could scarcely breathe.

"Look," he went on. "Whatever it is, don't let it get to you. We'll talk. Don't worry, sweetheart, I won't let you down. And don't worry about how it looks. What have I always told you about that? Let 'em talk about you and give somebody else a rest." Another pause. Amanda knew the caller was female and she could tell they were close, which sent a pain through her soul that threatened to rip her body in two. It wasn't that she hadn't thought he'd have other women in his life. It was that she hadn't thought it would matter so much.

"Hey," he continued sweetly, his approval evident. "I think you're finally beginning to see where it's at. Maybe there's some hope for you yet, old girl!" Another break as he listened. "Sure, next week is fine. You don't think your dad will go crazy on me?" And again, he paused. "Okay, then. If you're game, I am. Kiss your mom for me. Bye."

He got back into bed and wrapped his long arms securely around her. She snuggled against him, but the magic was lost. Every bit of pleasure, every ounce of hope, had evaporated.

"Who was that?" she dared to ask, hating herself as she did.

"Jealous, are you?" he teased, and her eyes filled with tears. "Hey . . . hey, don't do that," he coaxed. "Come on, now. It was just my little cousin."

"It doesn't matter." Amanda wiped her tears away quickly with the back of her hand. "I have no claim—"

"Oh, stop it. You stole my soul the first time I saw you and you know it." He pulled her close again. "Now listen. My cousin—well, she's got a little problem she needs some help with," Will said, as if unsure whether he wanted to explain further.

"What kind of problem?"

"Oh, you know—it's not even worth talking about, it's so silly. She gets herself involved in the damnedest things, and then blows it all out of proportion. I promised to help her out and I'll tell you all about it as soon as I can get my head around it. It's actually kind of embarrassing for a left-wing radical subversive like myself."

It was clear that was the most he was going to tell her, so Amanda kissed him, long, slow, and so earnestly he pulled away, surprised, and looked at her—but only for a minute. She wanted him again, as never before; and within a very short time, he wanted her too.

She thought he was probably lying about the phone call. There was no cousin with a silly problem. It broke her heart because he had no reason to lie. But she wouldn't make an issue of it. Instead, she would enjoy as much of him as she could in the time allotted to her.

For Julie, the days passed quickly—too quickly, and nothing happened. No cramps, no staining, and no period. Absolutely nothing.

It was bad enough having to wait, but she had come to depend on Amanda to share some of that burden with her. And Amanda had suddenly taken to staying out for entire weekends at a stretch. This was the second one in a row. She never said where she was going or when she'd be back.

Julie cursed herself for being such a child, even as she pouted and shuffled around in their little room. If only she'd been remotely interested in other people once in a while, she might know where to reach her roommate. If she had any clue where Amanda spent her free time, she would have called and begged her, if necessary, to come back to the dorm. It was the seventh day, for heaven's sake, and still nothing. Julie thought she would collapse from anxiety.

She had accepted a couple of dates and had tried to keep them, but ended up canceling at the last minute. She simply could not stand one more campus jackass preening as he showed her off at hangouts where people who mattered were likely to gather. At first it was fun, because she wanted Forrest to see her happy and out and about; but she'd only run into him once and he didn't seem to care. And the pretentious campus apes who took her out felt called upon to prove to her what good lovers they were, whether or not she expressed any interest in finding out.

She couldn't have been less interested, so she had no idea why she let some of them get get as far as taking half her clothes off before she asked them to stop. She seemed outside her body, and what they were doing to it had nothing to do with her.

So last night, she had dumped her date in the middle of dinner at the Floridian Hotel restaurant, one of Tallahassee's most popular establishments, to return to her dorm room alone. Josh, Forrest's friend and fraternity brother, was (in his own mind) entertaining her with tales of their daring escapades. She'd thought dating Josh would increase her chances of running into Forrest so she could rub his nose in it, but she'd been downright bored.

When it came to her like a revelation that she was reduced, out of spite, to dating brothers in the same fraternity, she had laughed out loud. Josh looked at her, surprised, for her laughter was bitter and hard and apparently in the wrong place for the story he was telling. That made her laugh even more.

She had choked down her salad and three of his off-color jokes, and it was just too much. The blue cheese dressing was too thick for her liking, and his expressions were too blue for her taste. After her bout of uncontrollable laughter, she had simply put down her fork and looked at him with genuine sympathy. Then she got up and walked out. Just like that.

She didn't make any apology or excuse, and she didn't feign a headache. She simply got up and left.

He had tried to follow her, but the proprietor of the little restaurant had called to him to come right back and pay the bill. By the time he'd gotten away, she had called a taxi and was waiting out front.

"Where in hell do you think you're going?" he demanded.

"Back to the dorm."

"Well, what did I do?" he persisted. "Hey Julie, I know what's going on with you and Forrest, so don't get on your high horse with me. Come on back in and stop making a spectacle of yourself. Or would you rather go on up to the Wayfarer and get a room? You got nothing to lose now, so why don't we go take advantage of the situation?"

He had tried to put his hand up under her skirt, but she had slapped it away.

"Don't you understand?" she tossed over her shoulder as she got into the cab. "Don't any of you understand, Josh? I don't want to be with you or anybody like you. And all of a sudden, there are just so many of you."

That's what had made her pick up the phone and call her cousin the minute she woke up Sunday morning. He was strong, and so understanding, as she knew he would be. She might even tell him about being pregnant. He might know what to do if the shots didn't work, and she knew she could trust him not to tell her mother.

The telephone rang, and for an instant she thought about not answering. It was probably that guy Jason again. He had called at least six times during the weekend, and each time she told him she would relay his message the minute she heard from Amanda. If he had the audacity to call at this hour, she would be tempted to give him a piece of her mind. But it was Amanda.

"For heaven's sake, where have you been?" Julie demanded like a petulant child.

"Do you want anything to eat?" Amanda ignored her question and asked. "I'm stopping off at the Sweet Shoppe before I come in."

"No," Julie said. "Well, maybe some coffee, if it's no trouble." She lowered her voice as if she'd been standing in a crowd and whispered into the phone, "Listen, I didn't mean to sound nasty, but well—nothing's happened yet, Amanda. Nothing."

"Don't worry. I'll be there soon."

An hour later, even before Amanda had time to put down her load of books and the containers of hot coffee, Julie repeated her bulletin.

"This is the seventh day, Amanda. And nothing. It's not going to work." She knew her voice was full of accusation, and she continued quickly. "I'm really sorry to bother you with it the minute you walk in. I know it's not your problem and I should be so grateful you're helping me that I could be more patient. But I just don't know what to do. I can't study. I don't want to go out. I'm just a nervous wreck."

"Have you felt anything? Any cramps?"

"Not even a pinch. And I keep running to the bathroom every five minutes to look." Tears of humiliation welled in her eyes.

"Well, he said about a week, more or less," Amanda tried to comfort her. "You'll have to hold on a little longer, that's all."

"And then what?" Julie's voice rose with a shrill edge. "Then what if nothing happens, Amanda? I don't think this is going to be enough, and I don't know what to do." The tears spilled out of her eyes and rushed down her face. The hours of lonely waiting and hoping had done irreparable damage to her psyche. Her voice small and shaky, she continued, "It's like a nightmare. I go to sleep depressed and disgusted and miserable, and I wake up feeling the same way. It doesn't end, it just doesn't end."

Julie hated herself for the display of emotion, but she could no longer deal with the horrible, smothering feeling, as if she would suffocate in her own despair. She sobbed uncontrollably, and it was a relief to cry—such a relief she never wanted to stop.

"Okay, that's enough!" Amanda commanded, gripping her arms firmly and shaking her. "You're not the first girl this has ever happened to, and you certainly won't be the last. Now stop it! It's not the worst thing that could happen to you, not by a long shot."

"But my life is over—"

"No, it's not!" Amanda cut her off and shook her again. "Now knock it off!"

Stunned, Julie stopped. She took a deep, shuddering breath. "I'm sorry," she whispered.

"Listen to me," Amanda continued. "This will be over with soon—one way or the other. Nothing is forever. Everything—good, bad, or in between—everything has a foreseeable end. Next year, you'll look back, and you'll hardly remember what any of this felt like, or what you were wearing, or what I looked like, or even what Forrest looked like." Her voice softened. "Somehow, it'll be as if none of it ever happened."

Julie allowed her roommate to pull her down to sit on the narrow floor space between their beds. Amanda handed her a tissue.

"I'm sorry, Amanda. Really," she repeated quietly, and she meant it. "After you've been so helpful, too. I didn't mean to attack you, honestly."

"Forget it. I didn't take it that way." Amanda opened her bedside table, took out a joint and lit it. Julie noticed her hands were shaking as she opened one of the coffees and gave it to Julie before she opened her own. "It's only been seven days. You can afford to wait another week, maybe."

"No, I can't," Julie said quietly, her voice breaking again. The insurmountable, nameless fear that had been haunting her for the last few days worked its way, finally, up from the shallows of her subconscious.

"What do you mean?"

"I'm three months gone now, Amanda, the best I can figure it. And once I feel it move—I don't think I could kill it, once I've felt it move."

Amanda considered in silence, as she studied Julie's face.

"You're thinking about having the baby?"

"No." Julie struggled desperately to keep from crying again. "At least, I don't think I've thought about it. Oh, Amanda, I wouldn't wish that on any poor little baby—me as a mother! Besides, I hate Forrest so much, I really—well, I just can't see myself with a baby, you know?"

"You could put it up for adoption, then."

"There has to be something else, Amanda. There just has to be. I can't do this to my folks. It'll just kill them."

"Somehow I doubt that. But okay. We'll go back tomorrow night. Andy said he knew one other thing to do. We'll ask him to do it. But Julie, if that doesn't work, you've got to tell your parents. It won't be so bad, once they get over the shock, and they'll know what to do.

No matter how hurt or angry they are at first, they won't let you down. And you know it."

Having Amanda around made Julie feel much better. She was so logical, so down-to-earth, so optimistic about everything. For one crazy moment, Julie envied her roommate, and wished that for a little while they could change places. Then she wouldn't have to worry constantly about what people thought. She could just do whatever she wanted, once she figured out what it was.

She dried her eyes, and as they drank their coffee and shared the joint, she told Amanda about her date with Josh, proud of herself that she was forsaking her old, empty way of life. "So where were you all weekend?" she finished.

"Oh, you know. I . . . ah . . . with a friend," Amanda said. "Nobody important."

"And even if he were, you wouldn't tell me, right?"

"Sure I would," Amanda answered, getting up to throw her paper cup in the wastebasket.

"Oh, I almost forgot," Julie announced as Amanda went into the bathroom and turned on the shower. "I finally did it! I finally asked someone to be my escort!" She paused, so that the announcement could have the proper effect. "Well, aren't you going to ask who the lucky man is?"

"Okay," Amanda called, closing the bathroom door. "Who?" Julie wondered if she was still listening.

"My cousin!" Julie called back, wondering if Amanda could even hear her above the running water, "Won't that be a joke on all of them?"

Julie felt calm, and suddenly very sleepy. She'd forgotten to tell Amanda about Jason's calls; but before she got into bed, she placed the scribbled messages on Amanda's pillow so she'd see them when she'd finished her shower.

Chapter Fourteen

It had not been an easy day. The more Amanda tried to push thoughts of Will and the weekend they'd spent together—and that terrible, ominous phone call—from her mind, the more they pushed at her. She shivered. It felt like a splinter under a fingernail, only it was pressing relentlessly into her brain. She started to read her term paper over again, for the third time, intending to concentrate if it killed her. And for the third time, she read her own prophecy in Dickinson's words:

I felt a funeral in my brain,
And mourners, to and fro,
Kept treading, treading, till it seemed
That sense was breaking through.
And when they all were seated,
A service like a drum
Kept beating, beating, till I thought
My mind was going numb.
And then I heard them lift a box,
And creak across my soul,
With those same boots of lead, again.
Then space began to toll

As all the heavens were a bell,
And being but an ear,
And I and Silence some strange race,
Wrecked, solitary, here.

Impatiently, she closed her notebook and recapped her pen. Whether or not her interpretation of the poems she had selected made any sense at all, it would have to do. She smiled cynically. If her English professor would not forgive her, she was sure Emily Dickinson would, considering her present state of mind. She checked her watch and then called to Julie, who was soaking in the bathtub.

"You'd better get a move on. I told Andy we'd be there at six."

She wished she had not offered to take Julie back to see Andy. She couldn't imagine what he would suggest at this point. Considering the circumstances, she couldn't think of anything he could do—at least, not anything that would be safe—and she couldn't understand why Julie refused to tell her parents. A lovely, entitled only child, she was sure to get whatever she asked of them. So what if they fretted and fumed and lectured a little? They would come through for her. They would think of a way to extricate their beloved child from scandal and, ultimately, they would forgive her indiscretion.

"It's raining again," Amanda informed Julie as she came out of the bathroom wrapped in a towel. "So bundle up."

Their umbrellas vied for the right of way with a rainbow-colored kaleidoscope of other umbrellas. It wasn't a heavy rain, just one of the annoying steady drizzles so common in northwest Florida. Amanda knew her roommate was popular, but she was amazed at the number of people who spoke to Julie along the way, obviously seeking her recognition and approval.

It made Amanda a little uncomfortable to walk beside her, even though she was certain Julie had no idea how she made her living.

She held her breath, wondering what she would do if anyone they met recognized her. But, she reminded herself, Jason was the only client she had on campus. He was an ass but he wasn't stupid. She was sure he wouldn't give her away. What other people thought of her, if they thought of her at all, had never mattered to Amanda. Now, suddenly, it did. For some reason, it mattered what Julie thought of her.

Andy greeted them with his usual warmth, offering them coffee as they propped their umbrellas in the stand next to the door and took off their jackets.

"No, thanks," Julie said. "I'd just as soon get it over with. That is, I guess Amanda told you—"

"Yeah. Nothing happened yet." He shrugged his shoulders. "I wish I knew how to help you."

"You said there's something else you could try," Amanda said.

"Well, I do. But it's sort of drastic. I'd really rather not do it."

"Please," Julie insisted, her voice half agony and half rage. "I'll try anything. Please. You've got to do something."

"What is it?" Amanda demanded quietly, reserving her judgment until she had heard the form of treatment.

"Okay," Andy said, tension registering in the line that formed between his bushy eyebrows. "I guess it sounds worse than it really is. I did it for my girlfriend once with complete success. You've probably heard it referred to as the old coat hanger trick. The main thing to be concerned about is sterilization, which is a simple enough process."

"How is it done?" asked Amanda.

"Well, we straighten a wire coat hanger, sterilize the end, which is then inserted into the uterus through the cervix. Then I would move everything around—you know, break everything up, so to speak. If it works, the uterus should start to contract and expel the dead matter within a few hours, a couple of days at most. It's like an induced, natural miscarriage, rather than an abortion."

"Where do you want me?" asked Julie. "Let's get started."

"Put your coat on," Amanda ordered quietly.

"I have to get this over with. I'm going to let him do it."

"Like hell you are. Do you want to kill yourself, and ruin Andy's life? He'd be arrested for murder. Now put your coat on." To Andy, she said, "I appreciate your efforts, and your good intentions. But you ought to have your head examined for even suggesting such crap!"

Amanda didn't wait for him to answer. She grabbed Julie's arm and pushed her out the door before she had time to protest further. It infuriated Amanda that someone who claimed to be her friend would dare to suggest butcher's methods to another of her friends.

When they were well away from Andy's, she stalked into the darkness ahead of Julie, who was dragging the white umbrella along the dank, leaf-strewn sidewalks. The noise it made grated on Amanda, and she turned quickly to see Julie's trench coat open and her scarf whipping in the raw, autumn wind. Tears were streaming down Julie's face, and her shoulders heaved spasmodically.

"Oh, for heaven's sake," Amanda said impatiently as she walked back to join her roommate. "Now get yourself together. It's going to be all right."

She reached up and buttoned Julie's coat, and a sudden, bitter memory surged vividly through her mind. Once when her mother had gotten a little tipsy, she had fallen and gashed her head in her efforts to give Amanda a beating. It was only a surface wound, but it had bled profusely, and her mother was almost hysterical. Amanda remembered herself at nine, reaching up to button her mother's fraying old sweater.

"I'm sorry," she had said, crying while wiping the blood away and feeling so totally responsible. "I'm sorry. It'll be all right, Mama.

It'll be okay."

Well, maybe she was a bit sick and tired of feeling responsible for the world and all its ills.

"I told you. Nothing is forever," she comforted Julie in a gentler tone.

"What am I going to do?"

"What you should have done in the first place. Tell your folks. Soon, and get it over with. Now come on. Let's get out of this wind. I'm freezing."

Julie trudged along beside her for a few moments, in thoughtful silence. Then she said slowly, "Okay. I guess you're right. She stopped and turned to Amanda. "But only if you'll go with me."

"Oh, come on, Julie. I don't even know them. Why would you want me to go? Don't be silly."

"Amanda, please don't make me face them alone. You've got to come." The panic rising in her voice made Amanda wince. "If you won't go with me, then I'm not going to tell them. I can't. I'll have to go back and let Andy use the coat hanger."

"All right," Amanda agreed despite her reluctance. "You don't have to blackmail me. But don't expect me to do the talking. Any of it. I'll go with you, but you have to tell them."

When they walked into the dormitory lobby, the receptionist signaled to Amanda. "You've got messages waiting," she called out. Amanda waved back and turned to Julie.

"You go on ahead," she said. "I'll be up in a couple of minutes." As Julie headed for the elevator, Amanda walked over to the desk. The switchboard operator held out two pink slips with one hand and plugged somebody in with the other.

"Mandy," begged the first scribbled note. "He's so tense he's bouncing off the walls. Please call." It was from Jason.

The second message was from Will. It informed her he'd be in the sweet shop until about nine, and he hoped she would join him for coffee. She closed her eyes in silent benediction to some invisible force that seemed now to be controlling her destiny. A smile played gently over her lips as she strode toward the elevator, her confidence and good spirits renewed.

She stuffed both messages into the pocket of her raincoat. He was so matter-of-fact about their relationship; and she was ready to concede that perhaps he was sincere. She had never thought it would be good for any man to take her for granted but she found it completely delightful.

"Why are you grinning like the Cheshire cat?" Julie asked drowsily as Amanda came into their room. She was lying on her bed fully clothed, her head cradled in her arms.

"Because the world is right side up for a change," Amanda said, tossing her books on the bedside table. "I have to go out for a while. You'll be okay?"

"Yeah . . . I'm good," Julie mumbled. "Go—have fun. I want to sleep. I just want to sleep forever."

"Okay. Get some rest." Amanda went into the bathroom and splashed water on her face. No, she thought joyfully. I don't have to go out. I want to go out. I am going to be with a man of my choice, because I want to be with him. And only him.

Without taking time to remove her raincoat, she combed her hair and started to put on some blush before she noticed her cheeks were already rose tinted—maybe from the brisk autumn air. Or could it be renewed hope?

The rain had slacked off, fortunately, for Amanda had forgotten her umbrella in her rush to get to Will. It was already past eight o'clock. At first, when she walked into the Sweet Shoppe, she didn't see him. Then spotting him at a table in the back, she breathed a sigh of relief. Her only thought, strangely, was that he was so tall. Seated, he was still head and shoulders above everyone else in the room.

He was having a serious discussion with a man in the adjoining booth, and she stopped for a moment to watch him, savoring anew the feeling of peace and contentment sweeping over her at the mere sight of him. She had to smile.

She had been with so many men so often she had lost count. Despite her mother's teachings that it was evil, Amanda liked sex and she had the rare ability to lose herself in a fantasy even when she was getting paid for her services. She had experienced the delights and peculiarities of the male designation in every form conceivable, yet when she looked at Will, even from a distance, she felt like she was drowning, submerged in deep fathoms of longing she had never thought possible. There was no joy, she thought, to equal that of his body sinking slowly into hers. There was no agony compared with that of his presence withdrawing from her.

She squared her shoulders, almost as if to meet a foe, and walked toward him. His beard brushed her face as he rose to kiss her. She shivered.

"Cold?" he asked, concern in his voice.

"No," she said. "I think it's stopped raining."

How could she tell him that seeing him again had sent tremors through her? And why on earth did she say such stupid things when she was with him?

He got her a cup of coffee and a cruller. She merely toyed with the pastry, but she gratefully swallowed the coffee, even though it was hot and too strong. They talked, and he smiled at her, locking her eyes in his own warm gaze all the while. She tried to enjoy the sheer pleasure of being with him, with no thought of yesterday or tomorrow. Instinctively, however, she braced herself, as if she had some kind of premonition.

"I have a little unpleasant news," he said finally, when they had lapsed into a brief silence.

"Really?"

"We won't be able to get together for a few days."

"Oh? What's up?" She tried to sound casual but her soul collapsed, and fragments of it landed with sharp, individual stabs of pain in the pit of her stomach, where they ran together in a solid lump. The lump lay there heavily for a few seconds, before she could summon up the courage to face what she had feared most since meeting him. The polite solicitude, the cautious but firm ending.

"You remember, I told you my cousin needs my help?"

"Yes. But you didn't say with what."

"I have to take her to—this big deal thing. She's somewhat of a social butterfly. Anyway, it's kind of stupid, and I'm not sure I want to be shanghaied for this kind of duty call. But she's a sweet kid, and I can't turn my back on her, especially now that she appears to be joining the real world."

"Of course not," Amanda said, her voice barely a whisper. "I understand."

She understood nothing except the thick, leaden weight slowly filling her. He reached across the table and squeezed her hand.

"Thanks—" he started, but she broke in.

"And then," she interjected mechanically, "you'll be leaving town at the end of the term."

"Before that, I guess. But we'll have time before I go. I'll make time."

She felt obliged to finish the cruller, but she couldn't force it down. Somehow he had found out about her, about what she did to make money. That had to be it. If only she could make him understand why. But she couldn't, when she didn't understand it herself. He had written books to keep from going hungry. She had sold her body—and her soul. At least, she thought, if he was ending it he was trying to be gentle. She should take some comfort in that, in his kindness.

She didn't blame him for breaking it off with her. It was just that the void returned to her life as suddenly as it had vanished. She wanted to talk to him, to try to explain why she did what she did (as if it were possible), but she didn't dare for fear she would cry. And she wouldn't cry—not for him or anyone. She wanted to go with him to his apartment and make love to him just once more, but she was too proud to suggest it. When he did, she declined with the excuse that she had to study.

He stood with her when she rose to leave, and she accepted his kiss; and then she shouldered her purse and walked out into the lightly falling Tallahassee rain.

Chapter Fifteen

Tom stared morosely at the yellow tip of the felt highlighter pen. Yellow. He had always hated yellow. It was the color of his room at home. Nice and bright and sunny, his mother had said. And the sunlight shining into his room and glaring from its walls into his eyes had always seemed to blind him. Yellow. It was the color of the dress his mother had worn to his high school graduation. He was valedictorian, and she had been so proud—as if she had done it all herself. He remembered the yellow lace bobbing up and down on her heavy bosom as she had applauded him. It was the color of lemon custard, which he hated. It was the color of his own skin sometimes. It was the color of urine. He closed his history book, recapped the pen and threw it in the garbage.

He had seen most of the kids in his English class—even Julie—marking their textbooks with yellow markers. Imitating them had not given him any sense of belonging. None whatsoever. He was nothing like them, nor did he want to be, not really. He was superior in intellect, if not in looks; and he firmly believed intellect would take him further in the long run.

He had always approached books with a certain sense of reverence, and it didn't sit well with him to be marking them, even if he had paid for them and could do with them as he pleased. What he pleased was to take copious notes on blank graph paper, to make methodical outlines as he had always done in high school.

He wanted to call Julie, but he knew she wouldn't have time to talk to him with Homecoming so close. He would be perfectly willing to wait for her, if only this girl of Jason's would call. This prostitute of Jason's, he reminded himself, because the word excited him. Someone who would be paid to let him put it inside her and pump up and down to his heart's content. Thinking about it tempted him, but he'd made up his mind to control himself. To wait for the real thing. To actually be inside a woman instead of giving himself a brief satisfaction in the shower. A satisfaction that was not much of a satisfaction anymore.

He was anxious to do it with a real woman and not one he imagined—but not only for himself. He had to know how to satisfy Julie when the time came. And from what Jason said, this girl—this paid woman—this prostitute—could teach him.

He'd started to undress for his shower when the phone rang. It was sure to be one of Jason's myriad Twinkies, so before Tom answered, he got the message pad ready.

"Hello," he said a little gruffly, annoyed at being personal secretary for a man who seemed to have more girls than he could handle.

"May I speak to Jason," a soft, feminine voice asked.

"He's not in," Tom recited mechanically into the receiver. "May I tell him who called?"

"Yes, would you please? This is Mandy. Is this Tom?"

He almost dropped the telephone. It was she—the girl. The prostitute. Where in hell was Jason?

"Uh, yes. I—uh—I've heard so much about you." God, what a stupid thing to say to this girl, this woman who took money for sex. She didn't seem to mind, though.

"Look, Tom," she said in a voice that reminded him of warm honey. "I've got some free time this evening, if you and Jason would like to meet me. Jason knows where."

"Sure. We would." Tom managed to make his voice steady. "As soon as he comes in, I'll tell him. How how long will you be there? I mean, I don't know exactly when he'll get back."

"Well, he knows how to reach me. I'll hang around there for a couple of hours. See you."

Tom replaced the receiver in its cradle and shook his head. Shit. Where could Jason be? He wondered if he'd sounded like an idiot on the phone. Why didn't he suggest meeting her himself? Damn it. Because Jason had the money and the grass, that's why. And part of the deal was that he be allowed to watch. Damn. Tom picked up his history book and threw it at the bed.

He decided to take a shower anyway. If Jason did get back in time, he at least wanted to be clean. He wondered if she would be. Oh god, he hoped she was—and that she wasn't ugly. He heard the door open and then slammed shut as be stepped out of the shower.

"Hey, Jason, is that you?" he yelled.

"You expecting Raquel Welch, maybe?"

Tom stuck his head out the door. "She called, Jason. Mandy called. She said you'd know where she'll be, and she'll wait for us."

Jason grinned. "Perfect timing, my man. I just picked up two ounces of the most unbelievable smoke. One for us, and one for the little lady. Well, what are you standing there for, with that glorious big dick hanging out? This is your moment, buddy. Get dressed. I know you're anxious to get laid, but we gotta get there first."

Tom chuckled, but in the privacy of the bathroom, he had to take several deep breaths to steady his nerves. He was going to lose his virginity at last. He couldn't imagine what it would feel like.

In the car, he wished he was calm enough to have a conversation with Jason. It seemed the least he could do. But Jason didn't seem to mind the silence, or to notice how tense Tom was.

"So . . . what does she look like?" Tom asked at last.

"Oh, she's cool. You'll like Mandy," Jason reassured him glibly. "She's outta sight, and she knows what she's doin' all right."

"That's good. But . . . what does she look like?"

"Don't worry. She's no bow-wow. Small—like petite, you know. Brownish hair, kinda shoulder length, I guess. Always smells real good. The perfect manicure, the full-out pedicure, you know—the whole deal. Puts herself together well." He laughed. "Nope. Nothing cheap about her. She's got class. And she has the same room every week at the Wayfarer Motel. It's like her home away from home. They don't even consider giving it to anyone else. You scared?"

Tom winced. "I don't know. Maybe a little."

Jason laughed, "I was too, the first time," he said. "Scared shit-less. My old man took me to a hooker he knew down in the Village. You know—Greenwich Village in New York? She was kinda old—but man, she was something. Did things to me I didn't know could be done. Experience is the best teacher. Right?"

"Obviously. How old is Mandy?"

"Old enough, my man. Old enough."

Jason parked the car and looked in the rearview mirror for a moment, scoping out the parking lot. Making sure there were no cops around, Tom thought. Then Jason pointed out her room.

"She's waiting right in there, my boy," he said as he got out of the car. "So let's get down on it."

Tom followed, and when they reached her room, Jason knocked lightly on the door.

"It's open," a soft voice called out to them.

They went in, and Tom could not believe his eyes. The young woman on the bed was small; and though a sheet covered most of her, he could see by her delicate shoulders and the slight curve of her bosom that her skin was all ivory and roses. She was slender, and young, and pretty. She wore no makeup except a little blush and maybe some mascara, and a sprinkling of freckles graced her slight, turned up nose. She looked like any average college girl.

"How ya doin', Mandy?" Jason boomed at the lovely creature, and Tom put his hand out as if to stop him. Mandy turned her eyes on him, and he became achingly aware of his every movement.

"Want to smoke first?" asked Jason.

"It's up to Tom," Mandy said quietly, in the same soft voice, as she smiled slowly at him. "It might help to relax you," she said to Tom. "I'm going to, but don't feel you have to if you'd rather not."

"No, I'd like to. I mean, I never have, but I guess I'd like to try some." He meant to do everything she suggested.

Jason took the necessary paraphernalia out of his shoulder bag. He sat down on the bed with Mandy and took the phone book from the shelf beneath the nightstand. Using it as a lap table, he sprinkled a generous helping of marijuana on it and began to roll some of the funny little cigarettes. Tom wondered what to say next.

"Would you like me to help you get undressed?" Mandy suggested.

"Oh, no. I think I can manage."

"The bathroom is right behind you," she said gently.

"No, that's okay. This is fine." A little dazed, Tom started to strip but he was relieved. So far, it was easy. It didn't seem at all unnatural or awkward, not even with Jason in the room. He couldn't take his eyes off the girl. She was nothing like Julie, of course. She was much smaller, and not quite as pretty. But she was something else. Not in the least what he had expected.

"Listen," Amanda said to Tom as Jason handed her a joint. "Don't expect anything much the first time. I don't want you to feel embarrassed, or anything like that, if you come right away. Men usually do the first time. Even when they're experienced, they usually come right away with a girl they're not used to. And if that happens, don't worry. We'll have another go. And if you like, I have something that will prolong it for you a bit, the second time."

"Oh, wow," Jason exclaimed with appreciation. "You brought some rings?"

"One," she said pointedly. "The deal was that you get to watch, remember? Nothing else. So keep your pants on and find yourself someplace else to sit."

Tom stood before the girl, his task of undressing complete; and he wished fervently for pockets. He could not imagine what he should do with his hands, or the rest of him for that matter. She offered the lumpy, strangely shaped cigarette to him, and he took it.

"Well, what do you think?" demanded Jason, and Tom almost answered before he realized Jason was talking to the girl. "Is he hung?" Jason persisted. "Or is he hung? What did I tell you?"

"Yes, very nice," she said and smiled up at Tom. "Why don't you sit here?" she added, pushing the sheet down around her ankles and patting the bed beside her. She was wearing lacy bikini panties so thin he could see her patch of pubic hair right through them. They looked like they would melt if he breathed on them. She was wearing nothing on top, and her small, perfect breasts were lovely.

She slid gracefully to the far side of the bed, making room for him to join her. When he sat down, the warmth her body had left on the sheet caressed his backside, almost overwhelming him. Glad the joint he was holding gave him something to do, he drew deeply on it. The sweet, dry taste filled his lungs, and somehow the warmth in his buttocks merged with the warmth in his chest. He could hear heavy breathing behind him as Jason pulled a chair closer to the bed, but it was plain Mandy meant to ignore his presence. Tom decided to do the same.

He took another drag on the joint and a feeling of peace and contentment slowly crept over his body, and he almost forgot his roommate was there.

"Now," the prostitute said softly, when their smoke was finished. "Do you want to use the ring?" Her tone was gentle and filled with kindness. He wanted to touch her breasts but he did not know how to begin, and he wondered if he was supposed to ask permission.

"Yeah, man!" Jason encouraged jovially. "Try the ring. It's a gas."

"You don't have to," Mandy reassured him, as she seemed to read his mind. "Maybe the first time, you'd like it more if you didn't use anything?"

Tom nodded.

"Do you want the lights out?" she asked.

"Hell, no!" Jason exclaimed. "How am I supposed to see anything?"

"Jason, please be quiet, won't you?" she said, and Tom was amazed that she could sound so sweet and so in control at the same time. She gave Jason a withering look and turned her attention back to Tom. There was nothing he would have liked more, at that moment, than to have the room in darkness. But after all, Jason was paying for everything.

"I don't mind if the light stays on," he said with a slight shrug of his shoulders. "Really."

The girl nodded once, faintly. "Why don't you lie back now," she suggested sweetly, patting the pillow. He did, and ever so softly, she started to run her hands over his body. First his neck, and then she worked her way to his shoulders, and down his chest. Soon he felt relaxed. Damn, he thought. Too relaxed. Cautiously, he looked down his own long form. Nothing. His first time with a woman, and nothing. He leaned back on the pillow and closed his eyes. Shit.

"Open your eyes," she commanded softly, and so he did. She moved gracefully to straddle his legs, not even trying to cover her body as, poised on her knees, she arched her back so that her pelvis—

outlined through the panties—moved slightly toward him. She was close enough for him to reach out and explore her body with his hands but not so close it would be clumsy.

"Look at me, Tom," she told him. "Look at all of me."

He let his gaze travel from her lips to her breasts.

"Do you like what you see?" she whispered.

"Yes."

"Do you want to touch them?"

"Oh, god—yes."

She took his hands and guided them to her bosom, placing them over her nipples and then moving them in a slow, circular motion. "Like this," she said. "Women enjoy this . . . and be gentle. You should always be gentle with a woman, unless she tells you otherwise. Now look down. Look at me."

He looked. She was arching closer, thrusting her pelvis towards him, ever so slightly.

"Do you want to touch me down there?"

"Can I?"

"First, you have to pull my panties down."

He reached out and drew them down to the middle of her thighs.

"That's good. Just be gentle and that way it'll be good for both of us. Go ahead now. Try it and you'll see. You can touch me down there if you do it ever so gently."

He did as she instructed, sliding one hand down between her legs. With relief, he sensed he was no longer soft.

"Oh . . . that's very nice," she whispered. "You've got it." Slowly, she guided his other hand up to her breasts. "That's it," she whispered. "Gently. Do you want to put one in your mouth?"

He didn't hesitate. As she leaned closer, he opened his mouth to receive her gift, wondering how long he could control himself. God, he thought, she tastes like honey. And she smells like cinnamon baking on apples.

He had never been so aroused, not even in his wildest fantasies . . . not even when he imagined he was making love to Julie.

"Are you ready?" she asked.

"Yes."

She turned them, maneuvering herself beneath him so gracefully he never had to relinquish his hold on her. He didn't notice how she got her panties off but suddenly, magically, they were gone.

"Now, Tom," she said. "I want you to feel something, so give me your hand again." He obeyed, unquestioning. She drew it down between her legs, opening herself to him and placing his middle finger between her nether lips. "Right there," she continued. "This is a woman's primary point of pleasure. If you satisfy her first, she will want you again and again. Would you like to watch me? Can you wait for that? It won't take long now."

"Yes . . . I'd like to, very much," he said politely.

Jason stirred, and Tom heard him shifting his weight uneasily, but his presence didn't matter anymore. Tom hung heavily between the prostitute's legs, bursting with a desperate need. He wanted to go crashing into her, but she seemed so small. And he had never seen a woman's face in orgasm. They didn't show that in any of Jason's magazines and Tom had never seen any pornographic films. And he wanted to see it all. He wanted this experience to last as long as it could.

"Okay," she said. "Keep going. I'll tell you when to look at my face."

She kept her hand on his as he stroked her and he was surprised to feel her grow warmer. He'd always been a quick study in everything he attempted, and this was no different. With her brief instruction, he now knew exactly what to do.

"Now, Tom," she said. "Now. Don't stop what you're doing down there, but look at my face."

Her face was beautiful in release. At first her eyes were closed and tension was etched across her brow, but then a pink flush spread from her neck, down her shoulders and up to her face at the same time. All the tension was washed away with that glorious color and she opened her eyes. Looking into them, he felt as if he was pulled into the eternity of space where he could become one with the stars . . . with the universe itself. And she was smiling. And he had done that to her. He had made that happen.

Slowly, she relaxed and he heard Jason groan. At last, Mandy spoke again.

"If you're ready, you should try it now."

He knew what she meant, and he was ready. She helped guide him as she arched her body up to meet his. She kept pressing, pressing firmly against him, until her flesh surrounded every inch of his. He groaned in ecstasy and exploded inside her.

She didn't move again until he had regained a reluctant consciousness. She held him tenderly and rubbed his back until he was once again aware of his surroundings. Then she got up and went to the bathroom.

He looked at his roommate. Beads of perspiration stood out on Jason's forehead and clung to his upper lip.

"Well?" Jason queried hoarsely.

"Yeah," said Tom, not knowing what else to say. He knew what achieving orgasm felt like. He'd done that before. But in his wildest fantasies, he had never imagined what a woman really felt like.

"This time, use the ring," Jason continued. "So you can stay with it longer."

She came back in the room then, so Tom only nodded. She was holding the plastic motel-room ice bucket, which she had filled with warm water.

"I'm going to give you a sponge bath," she said with a sleepy smile. "If that's all right. I just had a quick one so don't worry. I want to teach you something else women like."

"Yes," he said, wondering what was coming next. But he didn't care. He would do exactly as she said.

There was a washcloth in the plastic container and she used it to bathe his genitals as if he was a baby. "Here," she said, giving the ice bucket to Jason when she was finished. "Go and empty this."

When Jason came back from the bathroom, she held her small, incredible hand out to him, and he put another marijuana cigarette into it and lit it for her. Tom made room for her on the bed and she smiled congenially at him. He wished they could talk, but he supposed that was not included in the service. After they had smoked again, she reached her hand downward to grasp him. He drew in his breath, in surprise and pleasure, but he didn't move.

He felt almost paralyzed, in fact, and he thought perhaps the smoke was getting to him. He closed his eyes again, more to shut Jason out than anything else; and he felt himself floating as if on pools of silk.

"First, I'm going to do something to you," she said. "And then I want you to do it to me."

"All right."

"Now you should watch," she told him. He opened his eyes and incredibly, saw her take his manhood into her mouth. He had never dreamed anything could be so warm and soft. A new strength surged through him. Jason let out a heavy breath, but he didn't speak.

Tom felt himself go hard again.

"Now," she said. "Do it to me. Use your tongue."

He knew what she meant and the idea didn't repulse him at all, as he'd thought it would when he'd seen a picture in one of Jason's magazines. She maneuvered herself up his body and, holding on to the headboard of the bed, lifted herself to her knees, waiting for him to do as she had directed.

Leaning back on the pillows, he opened her with his hands, just enough to make a pathway for his tongue. As it made contact, she moaned and the muscles in her thighs tensed. Jason groaned again.

"Okay," the prostitute whispered. "That's enough." She slid down his body so she could mount him. As he entered her she put one hand on his chest for balance, and then she started moving up and down on him, stroking herself all the while, as he had done. He watched her, entranced, and it was an unbelievable sight. He made no sound. He couldn't. Before Tom knew what was happening, she collapsed on top of him, and he felt her flesh pulsating around his own.

This time, he found he knew what to do, and she had the good sense to remain passive and let him do it. Firmly, surely, he thrust himself into her, again and again. And again, he burst inside her.

Suddenly, Jason's rough hands gripped his bony shoulders and pulled him out of his haven. He landed on the floor and looked up in astonishment. Jason was standing naked above the girl. It was obvious what he intended.

"No!" cried Tom, and Mandy opened her eyes.

"Cut it out, Jason," she ordered. "We made a deal."

He didn't answer, and suddenly, he was on her. She drew her knees up to her chest and tried to fend him off with her fists, but she was no match for him. Neither was Tom. Jason was short, but muscular, and his raw lust gave him an unnatural strength.

He pinned Mandy's arms above her head with one hand and easily separated her legs with the other. Tom could think of no way to control him, other than getting a strangle hold on his neck. Jason turned his whole body sharply and drove his elbow into Tom's midriff. Then he delivered a blow to Tom's jaw, sending him sprawling across the room.

As Tom watched in horror, Jason pinned the girl to the bed once more and drove himself savagely into the sweet recess Tom had just left. Tom wondered why she didn't scream. She only stared silently at Jason with such hatred in her eyes that Tom didn't see how he could go on. When Jason was done, she pushed him from her in disgust.

"You lousy bastard," was all she said. "Get out and take your friend with you."

Laughing, Jason got up from the bed.

"Oh, come on, Mandy. You know you dig it. Besides, what's a guy supposed to do? There was no way I was going to walk out of here without gettin' some myself. You ought to know that by now."

"Just get out," she repeated. Tom started to dress. He wanted to tell her he felt terrible about what Jason had done, but he was helplessly mute.

"I'll leave some extra bread," said Jason, and Tom wanted to beat him senseless—if that was possible.

"And that should take care of everything, right?" the girl said cynically.

"It always does, man," Jason responded pleasantly. "Doesn't it?"

And Tom supposed it did. After all, she was a prostitute.

Chapter Sixteen

Jason's broad chest lay heavily on top of her own. He still had her hands pinioned above her head, and his perspiration was dripping all over her face. But this time, she was screaming. She could feel huge gusts of air filling her lungs, as agonized cries tore from her body.

With a start, she sat up and consciousness brushed the awful dream away. It was not her own cries she had heard, but the telephone screaming for attention. She propped herself on one elbow and reached for it.

"Good morning!" the desk clerk greeted her cheerfully. "How about some breakfast? Room service is no trouble."

Room service was practically unheard of at the Wayfarer, but this particular desk clerk was ever hopeful that a breakfast tray from a nearby coffee shop would give him an opportunity to sample the prostitute's wares. Amanda smiled wearily.

"No, thanks," she said. "Not this morning."

Her head was aching, for the nightmare still hung in her mind. She knew when she came fully awake she would have to deal with the reality of the evening before.

"Are you sure?" the desk clerk persisted, disappointment clearly in his voice. He had brought her many Sunday morning trays, and she knew that to him, merely being in the same room with her and musing at the goings on in there was enough for him to boast to his friends.

Many times he and Amanda had shared a cup of coffee and a couple of pornographic jokes before she had gone back to her little cubicle at the dormitory.

"I'm sure. Thanks, anyway. Another time."

She put the phone down quickly as the words caught in her throat. Another time. Another man. Not Will.

If she hadn't been so completely tripped out the night before on grass and tequila and drugs, she never could have gone through with it. She was hurt and bitter when she had called Jason and left the message with Tom. She had been almost eager to feel another man's weight pushing against her—anything to banish Will from her thoughts. By the time she had reached the Wayfarer, however, a new kind of dread had overtaken her. She had found herself trembling with revulsion at the thought of entertaining any other man with her special talents.

Blindly, she had smoked a joint and dropped a Quaalude. The first apprehension dulled, she did up the remainder of her meager supply of cocaine and took a couple of shots of booze. By the time Jason and Tom arrived, she was calm and relaxed and as pliant as her trade would suggest. The memory of the night before was vague and blurry for her now, but she did recall feeling sorry for Tom. He was frightened of the unknown, and she had felt him a comrade in some strange way. Jason she had refused to acknowledge until he had demanded her attention in his crude, savage way.

She tried to pull her thoughts together. Sunday morning and so much to do to prepare for Monday classes. She hadn't been able to study at all since Will's announcement that her brief reprieve was at end. Her schoolwork was horribly behind, and to make matters worse, she had promised Julie she would go with her to Sunday dinner at her parents' home.

As if to restore some life to herself, or some interest in living, Amanda sat up and rubbed her arms briskly. Gloomily, she surveyed the odious disarray around her. Unable to endure the mixed smell of two male bodies swimming beneath her all night, she had stripped the bed and tossed the sheets on the floor, where they still lay in a rumpled heap.

When Jason and Tom left, she had smoked another joint; and then, rather than falling asleep, she had dissolved into unconsciousness.

The grass hangover helped her make it through a tepid shower, which unfortunately cleared her mind. As she started to dress, a sudden memory of Will's long, lean body and broad chest surged against her protesting brain. God, she could almost smell the earthy warmth of his skin through his beard. She fell, crumpled in a heap, at the foot of the bed.

"Please," she begged, wondering who she was talking to. "Please, just this once! Please? Just one more time with him, and I won't ask for anything else. Ever."

The anguish shooting through her frame jolted her sharply back to her senses. She took a deep breath and let it out in a deep, cleansing sigh.

All right, then, she thought. So it was over. It had never really started, and now it was over. What had she expected? Nothing. And what had she received? Nothing. At least she was breaking even, so what did it matter? She had asked nothing, he had promised nothing, and their brief moment was now and forever, irrevocably over.

The only problem was, she knew deep inside her gut, that she had glimpsed what she had never imagined existed anywhere for anyone, especially for herself. She had fallen in love with Will, and the heart she didn't know she had was now splintered in jagged pieces around her feet. And there was nothing she could do about it. She finished dressing.

Heavy splashes of rain started to fall as she ran to her car. Regular torrents of it sheeted down around her as she pulled out of the motel parking lot and turned onto Monroe Street, heading for the University. By the time she reached Tennessee Street, volleys of thunder roared on the tail of the icy, rolling clouds wending their way over from the Gulf of Mexico. Lightning flashed so close to the car she was afraid to go on. She pulled into the haven of a Texaco station, and she watched, numb, as the storm raged around her.

It's like the end of the world, she thought morosely and wished it would be. Her mind wandered backward, to the scene the night before. She wondered idly how it would have looked to someone who was not taking part in it—the desk clerk, for example.

"The end of the world," she said dreamily, thinking of her mother and all the warnings she had received from her, warnings about roasting in Hell Fire and Damnation.

She watched as the puddles gathered around the car in miniature lakes and streams, and then rushed into the gutter at the edge of the sidewalk to pour relentlessly down the vast eternity of Tennessee Street. A sad, ancient feeling in her soul, she tried with some success to imagine a flood sweeping over the gates of Florida State University while a blazing curtain of brimstone fell on the gleaming white state buildings.

The end of the world. Obliterating life, hope, wishes, love, needs and desires. Obliterating the gnawing, aching cavern Will had left inside her. Deliberate or not, he had opened her up, rutted her soul with tender expertise, and then left her to lick her wounds in stunned bewilderment.

Craving him anew, she had a sudden urge to drive straight to his apartment and demand refuge in his strong and gentle arms. After all, she had not asked for this new emptiness. She had not sought him out. She reached for the ignition, but her hand froze on the key, unable to turn it. What if she went? What if she ran in, breathless from the wind and rain and the joy of seeing him, and what if he were in bed with someone else? Hell. She didn't think she could even deal with seeing him drink coffee with another woman.

She trembled and pulled her sweater close around her, but she knew she was not cold. A soft, strangling sound began in her throat and she clenched her teeth to hold it back. The rain poured around her in a powerful, fresh torrent and she sank slowly across the front seat of the car as great hacking sobs finally broke, threatening to tear her apart.

The storm gradually cleared. The afternoon turned sunny and warm, and the evening promised to be perfectly balmy. Amanda had always hated Indian summer, and one of the advantages of living in the South was that it hardly ever occurred. But when it did, it always left her with strange feelings of uncomfortable memories she couldn't quite recall, as though there was something in her life, some hurt, she should actively seek to forget.

She hid for the rest of the day in the library, not even bothering with lunch. She didn't know when she would be able to eat again. It didn't matter. Nothing mattered, now. Will was gone.

It always took Julie an unbelievably long time to get ready for a date, so Amanda was amazed to find her roommate dressed and waiting impatiently. She looked at her watch to find it had stopped.

"We're going to be late, and that's going to make Daddy a little angry," Julie said. She seemed more anxious than usual, and Amanda's sympathy for her surfaced anew. "You don't have to change or anything, do you? You look fine."

"Thanks—no. I'll just wash my face. Sorry I couldn't get back sooner."

For the first time, Amanda felt as though she should explain her whereabouts to Julie. To somebody. To herself. Thank God her time at the university was almost over, and she could get on with a real career. As she splashed cold water on her face, she resolved to put Will and any thought of romance or true love, or whatever it was, out of her mind and get back to work. Graduate school was out of her reach at the moment. She didn't have nearly enough money to get her through two years of grueling study. But she would have her BA and would be able to get a regular job.

Or, she considered, she could stay in school and pay for it the best way she knew how, the way she'd been doing it these last few years. Maybe that was her destiny. Back to her job at the bookstore, back to her books and back to her customers when she needed money. No more dreaming. No more wishing for something she could never have.

The icy water worked wonders for her, and with her resolution to serve only reality, she felt a calm resignation spread through her, covering her exhaustion like a salve, as she blotted her face dry. She could get by without love. She always had.

"Would you believe I was able to get gas," she told Julie, as she rubbed her cheeks briskly with the rough dormitory towel. "The line wasn't even that long."

"I've decided to tell them after dinner," Julie said slowly, and then laughed. "No sense in spoiling a good meal, especially considering the dregs we get here. I'll tell Mother, and then leave it to her to tell Daddy. She knows how to manage him. I don't know how she'll do it, but she'll find the best way."

Amanda knew Judge Carson's house, as everyone in Tallahassee knew it, for it was a luxurious showplace that had often been featured in the home section of the *Tallahassee Democrat.* But of course, she had never been closer to it, the few times she had driven through the most exclusive section of town, than the hedge that stood sedately at the road, guarding the grounds protectively behind its maternal green bosom. It was all she could do to keep from gaping in awe as she actually went through the hedge and approached the polished granite and marble portico. She was so tense the sight of a blue and silver bicycle in the driveway hardly registered. The house was grand—impressive, even. Its ivory pillars stood like tall, majestic sentinels, and stretched the height of the three levels. Despite its cool reserve, the exterior only hinted at the magnificence within its walls.

Houses like this are only in films, Amanda reminded herself. Real people don't live in them. There is nothing behind that exterior but the vacant lot at a crumbling old movie studio. It couldn't be real. She was at a loss as to where to park the car until Julie pointed out the carriage-house garage at the rear of the grounds.

"It's Frank's day off, or he'd park for us," the girl informed her, and Amanda concluded that Frank was one of the servants. "You don't mind going in through the kitchen, do you?" Julie asked, suddenly concerned. "We have to park here, and it's a lot closer than going back all the way out front."

"Of course not." Amanda wanted to laugh, but she could tell Julie was getting more nervous by the minute. She had a bitter urge to say, "Mind? Of course, I mind. I always enter mansions through the front door, or I don't go in at all." But in deference to Julie's worry about offending her, Amanda let it go.

What she really wanted was to get this day finally over with, so she could work on getting through the next day and the next, and through the endless maze of tomorrows spreading out indifferently before her. Endless tomorrows with no Will, no more falling asleep in his arms, no more waking up with him.

The screen door moved noiselessly on well-oiled hinges, opening into a kitchen almost as large as the entire house in which Amanda had grown up. The floor sparkled an immaculate welcome, and the countertops competed with the floor in brilliance. No crumb would have gone unnoticed or untended; no drop of water or cooking oil would have dared mar the smug complacency of the room. The heavyset, black woman standing like a monarch over the stove would have seen to that.

"Hi, Adele." Julie said fondly. "Is that chicken I smell?" To Amanda she added, "Wait until you taste Adele's fried chicken. It just melts in your mouth."

"Well, it's gettin' cold now, thanks to you," the black woman said firmly, but in a voice too sweet to be a reprimand. "I've got my own family at home, missie. I can't be messing around here all day while you're out gallivanting."

"It's my fault," Amanda apologized. "She was waiting for me. I didn't realize . . ." Her voice trailed off when the cook gave a chuckle.

"Don't you worry about it. Now you girls get on out there to the table," Adele ordered. "I'll tell the judge you're finally here." She moved the platter of chicken out of Julie's reach. "Your cousin's already here. Came to try on that tux. Funniest thing I've ever did see. Him with all that hair all over his face." She chuckled, and her voice lifted slightly. "You can't even tell where the suit stops and he starts."

"Oh, good," Julie said, leading Amanda into the dining room. "My cousin is a little strange, but you'll like him. You really won't be able to help yourself. He's quite a character. He and daddy don't get on well but Mama just adores him."

Julie was completely relaxed now, Amanda noted, comfortable and secure in the warm embrace of her home.

The dining room was as spacious as the kitchen and Amanda had to catch her breath at its beauty. The perfect floor was waxed to a high gloss, and sky-blue curtains graced shining windows so clean they looked as if they weren't there at all. An ornate mahogany buffet was already set with after dinner brandy, small crystal glasses, a silver coffee service, and a plateful of elegant little pastries. A huge oak table stood authoritatively in the center of the room, covered with snowy linen. Although the two massive pieces were totally different in wood and origin, they joined the corners of the room in an interesting, yet sedate harmony. The room was large, but not much else was required in the way of furnishings. The only other pieces were the eight chairs that matched the oak table, and a little stand in one corner that held about a dozen Hummel figurines.

Besides place settings for five, the table boasted a gigantic bowl of crisp green salad; delicate, crescent shaped rolls in a bun warmer; and a dish of chilled shrimp, studded with carrot and celery sticks. At either end of the table was a small china dish sitting on its own little mound of chipped ice, each filled with pats of butter in the shape of roses, complete with stem and leaves. Salt and pepper mills stood together near the head and foot of the table, and a bouquet of red and white chrysanthemums was the centerpiece.

A lovely, delicate looking woman was bent over the flowers, giving them a final rearranging. She looked up with a ready smile when her daughter swept into the room, and Amanda could see she had been one of those fair-skinned beauties whose looks fade quickly with the passing years, but whose grace and charm never do. Her beige wool dress was impeccable and her makeup and accessories as flawless as her hair, which though as colorless as her dress, was styled around her face in a perfect, wavy halo. She was much smaller than Julie, but there was no mistaking their kinship.

"My darlin', hello!" she exclaimed with a welcoming smile as she put one arm around Julie's shoulders. The other well-manicured hand was extended to Amanda. "How are you, dear? Julie just can't say enough wonderful things about you. I'm so glad to meet you at last." Her smile was sincere, and her dimples deepened a little in her greeting. Turning again to her daughter, she went on, "Honey, your daddy is just a teeny bit grumpy. Go and kiss him and put him in a better humor for our guest. We must get to the table before Adele flies off the handle and gives everything to the dogs."

Julie laughed and almost skipped out of the room. It would be all right, Amanda thought, once Julie told her parents of her situation. For girls like Julie, it would always be all right.

Amanda was more than uncomfortable at being in so sumptuous a house, and left at the mercy of this strong yet gentle creature who looked like no mother should look, whose lilting voice was soft and kind. To rid herself of the offensive nasal whine indicative, especially in the working class, of southern Georgia and northwest Florida, Amanda had taken a class in public speaking every term she could fit it into her schedule. When Julie's mother uttered the same syllables Amanda did (sometimes in a monotone to keep the redneck accent at bay), the sound came out as muted, tinkling wind chimes.

"That's the trouble, you know," Mrs. Carson went on, unmindful of Amanda's discomfort. "We see so little of her these days and when the judge is told she's coming, why he starts anticipating her visit hours before he should expect her. I try to make him understand how busy she is, but he absolutely dotes on her." She laughed her charming, musical laugh and added, "As if I don't!"

Amanda smiled, beginning to feel more at ease. "I guess she is kind of special," she said, finally understanding what made her roommate such an innocent little butterfly.

"Mrs. Carson," Adele announced, wheeling a serving cart through the door. "I'm going home as soon as I clear away for dessert. Before that, if everybody don't get on to the table and start eatin'."

Julie came through the door, arm in arm with her father. She was smiling up at him, and he was beaming down at her. Dusk was settling in, and the light from the chandelier played on the girl's glorious mane of golden hair, forming an aura around her that included the judge.

From a glance, one could tell theirs was a special kind of relationship. Amanda envied her for a moment, until the judge turned to greet his daughter's guest—and a slow, negative protest snaked thickly through Amanda's brain.

Oh god, no. Not him. Not one of them.

The names of her clients, especially the infrequent ones, never stayed with her for long, but Amanda never forgot a face. Since that first party so long ago, when she had been relieved simply to get through it, she had made it a point to study their faces. It was partly because memorizing their faces somehow isolated her from the acts she was committing; and it was also because she was curious. She wanted to analyze the character of these socially prominent and supposedly moral men in order to understand why they found the occasional company of a prostitute necessary.

Every detail of her encounter with the judge came flooding back to her. It had been late in her first year in the business—the spring of her freshman year. Her clientele had grown from the out-of-town legislators to include the less interesting but more regular trade of the local good ol' boys. County supervisors, some elected and some appointed, city officials, and heads of various county and city departments became her clients, and all of them referred customers to her. Some of them, naturally, were friends of the judge.

The mayor was by then a steady customer; and he had mentioned their once-a-month poker parties to Amanda, to see if she was interested in doing a group thing, for a very elite group. That month, he'd told her, poker night fell on the judge's birthday, so he had ordered up a royal celebration. Amanda and her partner were to arrive just before midnight, after they had played cards and enjoyed the buffet their wives had prepared. Amanda and Gunila, he said, would stay for only a couple of hours, since all the men would have to be home before dawn. And Amanda and her partner would have five hundred dollars to split between them. Not bad, she had thought at the time, for two hours' work.

Amanda could tell, when she had called the room from the lobby of the exquisite, old moss-draped hotel, that the men were slightly past the point of respectable intoxication. By the time she and Gunila reached the suite, the poker buddies had blindfolded the judge and were making him guess what his birthday present was.

Two of the men had silently motioned for the girls to disrobe. Since her partner was prettier and more buxom than Amanda, they motioned her forward and silently helped her onto the sturdy felt poker table, where they spread her legs apart before the judge, who was sitting there.

As the mayor removed the blindfold, Gunila propped herself on her elbows and threw each of her shapely legs over each of the judge's rotund shoulders. Amanda half expected the judge, whose harsh and puritanical reputation was well known, to rise in angry protest. He seemed delighted with the thoughtfulness of his friends, however; and with no hesitation he buried his thick, smiling lips into the womanly recesses between Gunila's thighs.

Amanda had been so amazed that she completely forgot what she was there for until one of the men grabbed her roughly around the waist and threw her down on the sofa as the others lined up for a turn.

In a semi-sitting position on the couch with her small feet resting tiptoe on the floor, she had been able to watch Gunila and the judge even as she moved in time to whatever response any of the other men wanted. Two of them were past their middle years, so with them, it was over quickly. The other two city officials were younger and stronger, however, and took considerably more time. They wanted to have her together, and they played their will upon her, trading angles whenever they chose. In less than five minutes, they too were satisfied; and when Amanda looked toward the table again, the judge still had his face buried in Gunila's silken folds, and Gunila was pleading for mercy. At last, the judge pushed his chair away from the table, and the mayor mounted Gunila. The judge watched, and as the client brought Gunila to orgasm (or at least, she pretended he did), he manually satisfied himself.

When the girls had dressed and the politicos had paid them and bid them a fond goodnight, the judge had told them if they ever needed any judicial aid, they should not to hesitate to call on him.

"How do you do, young lady?" The judge's voice pulled Amanda out of the memory. There was no trace of recognition in his eyes. "So glad you could join us. We've heard so much about you."

He hadn't been that drunk, and he had gotten more than an adequate look at her face, Amanda was sure of that. But it had been so long ago. She had gained a little weight, and her hair was longer. He saw so many faces each day, and hers was certainly nondescript enough. She relaxed. He seemed not to know her.

"All of it good, I hope," was her natural response to his greeting. "A pleasure to meet you, sir."

Adele had placed the main course on the table and was standing impatiently by.

"My, isn't it refreshing to find such respect in the younger generation," Mrs. Carson chimed melodically in the general direction of her husband. To Amanda she said, "Now, dear, you sit here by Julie. Adele, will you please call William one more time?"

The judge held Amanda's chair for her, and then saw to his daughter who he placed as close to his right as possible without making dining awkward. He left his wife to seat herself.

"No ma'am," Adele said with awesome dignity, as she removed her apron. "I've hung around this house long enough for one day. My James has his own tuxedo to see to, you know. Mrs. Carson, if I hadn't needed the extra money so bad, what with Homecoming and all, I wouldn't even be here today."

Heavy footsteps stormed downstairs, and a jolly, familiar voice rang in Amanda's ears.

"It won't do, Aunt Myrtle! It just won't do, unless you want your daughter to be the laughingstock of the year. In that getup, I look more like an eighteenth-century undertaker than a Homecoming escort."

He burst into the room, his white teeth showing through his black beard in a contagious, irresistible grin. He was wearing faded jeans, and he was tucking an equally faded shirttail into them as he came through.

Julie jumped up to welcome him with a big hug, and the judge bellowed, "William, we have a guest and you're late and half dressed! Sit down, if you please."

Mrs. Carson tried unsuccessfully to smother a laugh while Adele guffawed aloud. It was clear he was a favorite with the women of the household, even if the judge frowned at him with obvious disapproval.

"Come and meet my roommate," Julie commanded sweetly, as she led him to the table.

Amanda turned to him, unbelieving, and Will swept her immediately into his arms.

"What are you doing here?" he asked, laughing down at her, delighted.

"Do you know this young woman?" the judge demanded, his agitation at such dinner table behavior increasing with every syllable.

"Know her?" Will responded. "She just happens to be the most wonderful woman I've ever met in my life," he winked at Julie conspiratorially. "And I've met quite a few, if I say so myself."

"Oh, Will," Mrs. Carson entreated, eyeing her husband apprehensively while trying to make light of the matter. "Do stop your teasing. Come and sit down."

Dutifully, Will took his cue and helped Julie into the chair meant for him. Then he settled himself beside Amanda and looked respectfully towards Mrs. Carson. "There," he said in mock humility. "Will that do?"

"Quite nicely," boomed the judge. "Let's see if we can hold it down to a dull roar, if you please. I'm hungry. No thanks to you, my dear."

As the judge turned his attention once more to his daughter, Will pulled Amanda's small hand into his lap and squeezed it, looking fondly into her eyes.

Mrs. Carson folded her hands to say grace, but Adele had noticed the bouquet of chrysanthemums in the center of the table. With an exasperated sigh, she whisked them onto the serving cart, already taking the red ones out, even as she was wheeling them toward the kitchen.

"How many times have I told you, Miss Myrtle! You can't put red and white flowers in the same vase on a dinner table. It means a funeral around the corner. Only way now is to burn these red ones, as if I had time for all of that. My lord, you people going to be the death of me someday." On her way out she added, pointing at the flowers, "I'll take care of this mess and then I am leaving. I'll see you tomorrow." She would not even give them a backward glance.

"I declare, I can remember the respect Adele gave to my mother when I was a little girl," Mrs. Carson said wistfully, still in shock.

"How times have changed," mumbled the judge.

"I suppose for the better, though," his wife went on. "But you know, much as I love her, Adele does take sadistic pleasure in reminding me that her grandson is going to take part in the Homecoming festivities, the same as Julie."

Will looked up in surprise. "Is James going to be an escort? It's about time. What lucky girl got him?"

"Not an escort," the judge said gruffly, as if that were the most asinine thing he'd ever heard. "He's to be master of ceremonies. He is a talented singer—and dancer, of course."

"Of course," Will said dryly. "All his people are, you know." Julie giggled, and her cousin continued, "Julie, you missed your chance. You could have asked James and still kept it in the family."

"That will do," the judge admonished. "We have to move with the times, Will, but that doesn't mean we have to tolerate it in our social circle, or like it in the least bit. I hope you will apologize to Julie for that piece of tasteless humor."

"Oh, Daddy," Julie said, bestowing her Homecoming Court smile on her father. "The only reason I didn't ask James was because I didn't think of it." The judge almost choked, but Julie went on unheeding. "I'll bet he would have treated me with a lot more respect than all those goons who were working so hard to get me to ask them."

"Especially if he thought the men in the white sheets would be hot on his tail, if he didn't," Will responded pointedly.

The meal got underway at last, but Amanda found she could not eat. Her mouth was dry, and her throat constricted when she tried to accommodate the delicious looking morsels. She was stunned at finding Will there and even more surprised he was not lost to her after all.

It never occurred to her that Will could be related to Julie, of all people; and she couldn't dismiss the feeling of revulsion that suddenly hit her. She was ashamed as much for doubting Will as she was for the night she'd had before, with Tom and Jason. Will had been honest with her. The cousin wasn't fictitious, and he really did have to help her. She looked with disbelief from Julie to Will, but it was still difficult to take it in, even with them sitting at the same table. As Will passed the platter of chicken to her, Mrs. Carson's next words drew her attention.

"Still, Judge," she said, using his title instead of his name and speaking it almost as if it were a prayer. "Some things are not right morally, no matter how proper they might seem socially."

"For instance?" the judge treated his wife with a respectful disdain, as though he tolerated her presence merely because she was Julie's mother and because she looked so much like her daughter.

"Well, take the First Lady's Tea a few years ago," she replied and turned to explain to Amanda. "Every new governor's wife is the guest of honor at a tea held shortly after the inauguration." She turned her attention back to her husband. "You know when Governor Claude was in office his wife was treated miserably. Only three ladies, beside myself, attended the most exclusive social function of the inaugural season."

"You have to remember, Myrtle, that she was a foreigner, and she did break up his marriage to the first Mrs. Claude."

"Now, we don't know that for sure, Judge," she avowed in a small voice that grew smaller as she pressed on. "And you can't just treat people any old way because of some rumor you think might be true."

"My dear, you have a tendency to believe the best of everyone. I think if a prostitute walked in here with the letter A branded on her forehead, you'd swear her name was Alice, and that she was a perfect lady."

Will and Julie laughed at this unexpected witticism from the old man, and Amanda turned pale.

"Judge! Now you've shocked our guest. What will she think of us?" Mrs. Carson turned to Amanda. "Please forgive my husband," she implored. "Seeing Julie has made him so happy he has forgotten his manners." She looked reprovingly at the judge, blushing deeply. He did not bother to respond to her. "Julie," she went on, "Why don't you plug in the percolator and set out dessert while I clear away?"

"Can I help?" Amanda offered, wishing fervently for a temporary escape from the judge's presence. Will squeezed her hand again, and Mrs. Carson waved her back into her seat.

"Now you sit back and relax. Julie's told us how hard you work at the bookstore and at your studies. If she had half your ambition, maybe she could get a scholarship."

"Like she needs one," Will said, teasing his aunt. "As it is, FSU has offered us a tidy sum not to enroll her next year."

Julie laughed, thoroughly enjoying his attack, and Amanda detected a gentle conspiracy in their relationship. The judge frowned disapprovingly at them as they cleared the table and set out the dessert dishes.

The judge himself poured brandy for each of them, as Julie brought a large casserole of chilled banana pudding from the kitchen, together with a sweet, hot sauce Mrs. Carson had prepared earlier. Amanda watched her roommate going about the little domestic duties that obviously pleased her father, and she wondered what it was like to be so loved.

After Julie placed the elegant pastries next to the banana pudding and took her place again, she looked at Amanda and smiled. But as suddenly as the smile came to her lips, it vanished; and she quickly placed one hand across her abdomen. An odd look came into her eyes, and she grew suddenly quiet.

The gentle pressure of Will's arm on the back of her chair turned Amanda's attention away from Julie, but she couldn't help noting how restrained the girl had become, even as the judge tried to draw her out again. Finally, Julie became more animated, as if she had been turning some riddle over and over in her mind and had finally figured out the answer.

"I imagine the ladies would like to indulge in some girl talk about frocks for the dance, Will," the judge said at last. "Would you care to watch the football game?" His voice was strained and formal as he spoke to his nephew, obviously forcing himself to be civil. "The color set is a treat."

"It sure is," Will said and winked at Amanda. "Whenever you ladies are ready to leave, I'd appreciate a ride back to the campus."

"Of, course," Amanda said quietly, happily.

Amanda wanted to make herself scarce, to give Julie the opportunity to speak to her mother alone, but Julie refused to let her go. She engaged Amanda in meaningless conversation and directed her to dry the dishes while her mother washed. She would put the food away, and then sweep the dining room.

"Won't Adele be pleased when she doesn't have a thing to do tomorrow?" Julie said gaily, as if enjoying the chores.

When they had dried the last dish and Julie had put everything away, she bent to embrace her mother. "We really have to get back to the dorm and study, Mama. Don't forget we have to pick up my formal this week. Come on, Amanda. Let's see if we can drag Will away from the game."

Will was happy to be summoned. The judge said goodbye to Julie in the privacy of his den, so he did not feel it necessary to see them to the door, but Mrs. Carson kissed them all good night.

As they exited the house, the pungent smell of fresh flowers burning to ash invaded Amanda's nostrils. She looked toward the backyard grill where the red chrysanthemums smoldered, only half consumed by the fire that was almost out. Julie ran to extinguish them with some rainwater gathered, from the earlier shower, in a watering can.

As will strapped his bike to the top of her car, Mrs. Carson's words echoed in Amanda's ears: I hope you'll come see us again real soon. They seemed to accept her at face value, exactly as Julie had presented her—all of them, including the judge. And Will. Will was loyal and honest, as he had been all along. She drew in a deep breath and slowly let it out, her fear of losing him dispelled. Offering her keys to him, she said, "Why don't you drive—would you mind?"

He grinned at her. “Is that a sign I see?” he asked.

“A sign?” She was puzzled. Pleased, but puzzled. “What kind of sign?”

“The first indication I’ve seen that you’re ready to give up a little control. You’re not in this relationship alone, you know.”

Taking the keys, he bent to kiss her quickly before he got behind the wheel. She sat next to him, as close as she could get, touched and grateful for his open display of affection. So touched her happiness threatened to explode inside her. It was a relationship—he had said it. He considered what was going on between them a relationship. She was so filled with new hope she almost forgot about her roommate’s behavior, and not just at dinner. Julie was now leaning forward from the back seat, and Amanda saw a strange new light, reflected in the rearview mirror, in her eyes. Amanda looked back at her.

“You okay?” she asked.

“Oh, Amanda,” Julie said looking behind them to make sure they were out of sight of the house, as if she thought her parents would hear her even from this distance. “I felt it move. Twice!” She said the words as if she had to say them or burst.

“Really?” Amanda said.

“I know what I’m going to do now.” Julie’s face was shining, and her voice was light and happy. “I don’t know why I didn’t think of it before. I told you how I thought I’d feel if it moved. And I do. Only more than I thought. So much more!” She added quickly, “Oh, I’m going to give them Homecoming. They deserve that, I guess. Then I’m going to tell them. Not the details of course. But I’m going to tell them, and whether they help me or not, I’m going to keep it.”

“I hate to seem nosy,” Will broke in. “But would it be too much for someone to tell me what’s going on? Or do you want me to remain an ignorant bystander?”

“Just a small miracle, that’s all!” said Julie. “As miserable as I was last week, that's how happy I am now. I'm carrying life inside me, Will. I'm going to have a baby! Can you imagine what that's like?"

"I'm sure I can't," replied Will, smiling his blessing at her. "Are you sure this is something you want?"

"I am! It's . . . it's actually wonderful. It's another person. I've got someone to take care of—someone who'll need me and love me more than anyone else in the whole world."

"You're not scared anymore?" Amanda asked.

"Not as much as I was. It's so simple. It's natural, and right. And I'll do it—without the father. Other girls do. There's no reason I can't."

"Except the judge will disown you," Will said slowly, concern in his voice.

"For a while, maybe; but Mama never will," replied Julie, her confidence adding strength to her words. "She'll find ways to help me—us. Whatever happens, this has to be. It's what I want to do. What I must do."

She's right, Amanda thought during the ride back to the campus. It is a miracle, but not the only one. Sitting next to Will, as if completely belonging to him, to both the people in the car with her, she finally felt at peace. She had misjudged Will. She never would again and if he loved her as she now believed he did, she would never have another customer. That part of her life was over, and a new part was beginning. She took comfort in Julie's happy face, and she knew Will would help his cousin. She and Will would both help Julie, she amended, together. Because she had no doubt they would be together.

This strange new peace had nothing to do with Julie's decision, yet it had everything to do with it. It was the joy of a new life beginning for them both; and at the same time, it was the peace of coming home, of finally knowing where home was, and of belonging to someone at last.

Julie settled back and closed her eyes. Will reached across Amanda's lap and turned on the radio. He smiled down at her, his eyes warm and promising, as the Cascades entreated, *Listen to the rhythm of the falling rain . . . telling me what a fool I've been.* Amanda snuggled quietly against his shoulder and firmly dismissed the happy tears that threatened.

Chapter Seventeen

Julie pulled the covers more closely about her to ward off the early morning chill. Glancing at Amanda's empty bed, then at the clock on her bedside table, she sat up. She was supposed to meet Amanda and Will for breakfast, before the festivities of Homecoming Day got under way. The clock's hands refused to move any faster than their normal pace; and the gray light of dawn stubbornly procrastinated, indifferent to her eagerness to get the day underway. While she did not begrudge the lovers their newfound happiness, it was hard sometimes to be alone when her plans for her new life, and the life she carried inside her, assailed her every waking moment.

It had been exhausting—this, her last week in the ostentatious world of social propriety and obligation. Somehow, she had managed to get through all that was expected of her, banal as it all now seemed.

For a few moments she occupied herself with wondering what her child would be like, speculating on the possibility the baby might look like Forrest. The difference now was that he was superfluous, as if he had simply been some uninvolved, dispassionate donor—which was exactly what he had been, after all. It didn't hurt or embarrass her anymore, and if the baby looked like him, so what. According to Josh everyone knew anyway, so let Forrest be the one to tell people why he refused to take responsibility. Her version of the story would be that she had turned him down.

After looking at the clock again, she rearranged the pillows to support her back, which ached slightly. The baby also moved, as if to bid her good morning; and she tenderly ran her hand across the tightening skin of her abdomen. She gazed indifferently at her formal evening gown, hanging grandly on the outside of the closet door. Amanda had refused to let her cram it into her already stuffed garment bag for fear it would be crushed and unfit to wear to the dance. It glittered in the morning light.

Her mother had insisted on an ante-bellum style—white, of course—and low cut. The seamstress had copied the gown from the one Julie had worn in her last year of high school, the day she was crowned Queen of the May Court. If her mother had been puzzled when the seams of the dress had to be let out, she hadn't expressed her curiosity. Letting out the seams made the hemline fall unevenly, and Mrs. Carson wanted it to be taken out and redone. Julie managed to convince her it didn't matter. She wasn't planning to wear the dress after Homecoming.

"Well, of course, darlin'," her mother had responded sweetly. "You'll have another one for the Christmas ball. That's a must. And time is short after all," her mother had conceded. Julie had felt a quiet victory, a new kind of strength, as she reminded her mother about Will's beard. Julie knew if anyone could get him to shave it off, it was the strong and sweetly determined Myrtle Carson. If she didn't convince him to get rid of it completely, she would at least persuade him to give it a close trim.

Julie was glad she had asked Will to be her escort. She could not have tolerated for one instant some preening jock showing off and trying to make out with her at the same time. Her cousin was like her own guardian angel, and Amanda was as concerned about her as a fussy old hen. It was odd Julie had never thought of introducing them. They were perfect for each other.

And it was odd that she had never really seen people before, and that she had never taken the time to look. It was quite a revelation that others could have feelings as real as her own. Seeing her old friends through new eyes was an enlightening experience for Julie, as she watched each of them go through one display after another of carefully staged grandeur as they rehearsed for the homecoming game's half-time procession. At times she had been annoyed, but when she looked at Will, he only smiled benignly down at her, completely unimpressed by the whole exhibition.

After the round of parties, meetings, parades, and local news interviews on radio and television, Homecoming Weekend opened officially on Friday evening with a pep rally. Since the Homecoming court had to actively participate in the skit, Julie had insisted Amanda accompany them and sit in the audience with Will. She had even asked Amanda to go to the dance with them, but Amanda had refused, insisting that she would feel out of place.

"All that stuff—it's really not my thing," she had said.

When she continued to balk at the idea of going to the pep rally if nothing else, Will had insisted there was no way he could get through it alone. Amanda had finally given in. Happily, Julie had watched them from her position in the wings. Amanda looked uncomfortable and anxious, and Will drew her to him in a brief embrace. That was love, Julie knew—real love, and nothing like what she and Forrest had shared. Her relationship with Forrest, she now understood, had been more like a social contract. Who else would the football hero go out with but one of the most popular girls on campus? Oddly, the realization made her think of Greg Steinberg. Think of him and for some reason, miss him.

The Homecoming pre-game skit consisted of a lot of running and tumbling, since the queen and her attendants traditionally represented court jesters and buffoons from the Shakespearian era. They ran around the stage, falling on top of each other, cracking dirty jokes that were more innuendo than explicit and whacking each other with initiation paddles. By the time it was over, Julie was ready to collapse, and she would have been willing to return to the dorm with Amanda. However, her parents were close at hand, beaming with pride and anticipation of the party to follow.

As she stood in the receiving line with the queen and the rest of the court, still in their costumes and clown makeup, Julie saw Forrest out of the corner of her eye. He was standing in a huddle with some of his football friends and a group of Delta Zetas, the sworn enemies of her sorority. Although she had given him the ultimate snub of waiting until the last minute to choose her escort, thereby keeping him in limbo until it was too late for someone else to ask him, he was still very much a part of the inner circle.

A slight tremor, more of repulsion than anything else, went through her at the sight of him even though it was obvious all his flirting was for her benefit. Will steadied her on her feet, and then some of the other girls clamored for her attention. Gratefully, she had turned away and had completely forgotten about Forrest, relieved she would not have to share any part of her baby with the stranger on the other side of the room.

Her clock's alarm went off, startling her out of her reverie. She got out of bed and dressed quickly, a new feeling of energy surging through her. Since deciding what course her life would take, she had not felt the horrible nausea that had assaulted her on previous mornings.

Briskly, she brushed her hair and because she had neglected to set it in curlers the night before, it fell around her shoulders in an unruly mass. She quickly piled it on top of her head, clasped it and drew a small ringlet out to rest on either side of her face. Each curl caressed a cheek, and she smiled back at her reflection. She felt remarkably well.

Will and Amanda, holding hands across the small table, were waiting for her at the sweet shop. She greeted them with warm affection.

"You look radiant and dewy-eyed this morning," Will told her fondly as she sat down beside Amanda.

"I feel magnificent!" she announced. "Except that I'm famished."

"Stay here," Will said, rising. "I'll get it for you. What'll it be?"

"Umm, thanks. Bacon and eggs, toast, small orange juice—no, half a grapefruit—and tea with lemon, okay?"

"How do you want the eggs?"

"Fried soft, with grits. And extra butter!"

"Did I hear someone say you're eating for two?" he teased.

"Well, I haven't been taking very good care of myself," she said. "I think I have a couple of months to make up for. Anyway, I could eat a horse and a couple of small countries."

"We'll let you start with the bacon and eggs," Will responded cheerfully, still smiling as he headed for the food line.

"Aren't you running a bit late?" Amanda asked. "You must have slept past the alarm. You remember to set it?"

"Of course. And I woke up hours before it went off, and just couldn't go back to sleep. Oh, Amanda, I've never been so happy in all my life."

Amanda looked at her watch, a little troubled. "Well, I don't think you'll have time to go back to the dorm, by the time you finish your breakfast—"

"What on earth are you talking about?" Julie demanded good naturedly. "I didn't forget anything. I'm sure of it."

"Yes, you did," Amanda said with a big smile. "You don't have on any makeup. Not a drop."

Julie touched her face and then giggled. "I completely forgot! Do I look terrible?"

Her small white teeth sparkled between the natural coral of her lips, and her cheeks glowed in the morning light with the same hint of pink.

"As a matter of fact," Will said as he placed her tea and grapefruit in front of her, "I've never seen you look better."

He returned to the counter to wait for the rest of her order. She looked at Amanda for confirmation.

"It's true," Amanda agreed. "But what about the other girls? Won't they—"

"Oh, I don't care about them anymore," Julie interrupted. "You know what I've been thinking? My mother owns a house out near Silver Lake. It used to belong to my grandfather, and he left it to her when he died. Well, anyway, it's all furnished and everything. I'm going to ask Mama if I can stay there until the baby comes. My father doesn't approve of women owning property, so he never goes there. If she has to, she can always let him believe I've gone away somewhere. And you can stay with me out there, and Will can come and visit and he and Mama will bring us groceries. And I'll walk, and fish, and read and listen to music. Think of what a beautiful, peaceful baby I'll have. It'll be perfect. What do you say?"

"You're sure that's what you want?"

"Yes, absolutely," Julie insisted. "It's not so far to drive. You only have two early morning classes a week. And you won't have to pay, like you do at the dorm. Please—say you'll do it!"

"Somebody needs to look out for her," Will agreed, placing the tray before his cousin. "She can't be trusted to take proper care of herself."

Amanda shrugged. "We'll see." she picked up her coffee cup. "You guys better hurry. You'll be late."

Julie attacked her bacon with enthusiasm and mixed the eggs colorfully with the grits, which were cooked to just the right consistency.

"I don't know why we have to practice the promenade at all," she said. "It seems simple enough. They blow the whistle at halftime, the band will do their stuff, and then we march around so everyone can get a look at who's wearing what. Just like every year."

"Except that, this year, they know you'll be out there, and they want to make sure you march in the same direction as the rest of the court," Will said.

"Yeah!" Julie shot back and made a face. "And they know the absent-minded professor will be with me, and the dignity of the Homecoming Court will be in double jeopardy."

They all agreed that after the promenade rehearsal, Julie should have a light—this adjective heartily endorsed by Will—lunch and return to the dorm for a rest. The game would start at four, and since the dance was to follow immediately, the Homecoming court would leave the field directly alter halftime to change into evening clothes. Then at eleven, the girls were scheduled to go back to their residences to change for the midnight supper. The supper was an annual event, open only to the football team, the Homecoming Court, and their families.

Julie grimaced. "It seems I do more changing clothes than anything else. But it's almost over. This time tomorrow, I'll be finished with this nonsense forever." She trembled suddenly, and hurriedly placed the teacup back on its saucer with a small clatter.

That night, even though her stomach was churning from nerves and excitement, Julie enjoyed sitting quietly beside her cousin. With shared amusement, they watched the rest of the Homecoming Court cheer wildly, and then rise in unison at each crucial point during the game.

A dull ache had started in her lower back, so unobtrusively she was hardly aware of it. But by half time, she was in so much pain she hardly knew or cared what the score was. Will made some comment about the home team being ahead.

"Must be fixed, then," Julie mumbled, as he pulled her to her feet. The Homecoming court assembled at the edge of the field as the band performed; and on cue, Will led her out on the field so the crowd could pay their homage. She smiled past the pain, up at the spot where her mother and father were sitting. Gradually, as surreptitiously as the pain had come, it started to subside.

Julie swallowed some aspirin as soon as she reached her room. Her mother and Amanda acted as her ladies in waiting while she changed from the powder blue knit suit to her glittering white formal. By the time she finished dressing, the pain was gone.

A wave of premature nostalgia swept over Julie as she entered the brilliant, strategically lit ballroom on Will's arm. The orchestra was softly playing *Unchained Melody* over the chattering youthful voices, as students found their tables. This was the part she would miss, she thought a little sadly. The dressing up, the dancing, and yes—even the mass approval that seemed to be part of her birthright. But life goes on, people grow, and there comes a time to put away childish things forever. She sighed, almost inaudibly.

"Are you okay?" Will bent toward her, concerned.

"I'm fine," she said, smiling up at him. "Just a little tired, that's all."

He patted her hand. "Hang in there, kiddo. Only a few more hours until freedom."

She did not reply. She only squeezed his arm in return. The group seemed more or less assembled, and the master of ceremonies greeted the guests.

"Doesn't James look marvelous?" Julie teased, glancing at her father with a mischievous twinkle in her eyes.

"Yes—well, James was always a fine-looking boy" the judge

replied evenly. Will chuckled but Mrs. Carson turned pale, so Julie let it go.

James welcomed alumni, students and parents alike. After he introduced the Homecoming Court the orchestra struck up a waltz. The first dance was for the radiant queen, her attendants, and their escorts while everyone else watched from the sidelines. Julie released Will's hand and went to curtsy before her father. The judge beamed as he led her onto the dance floor. Mrs. Carson nodded her approval.

After that, prospective partners laid siege to Julie. For the first three-quarters of an hour, she hardly had time to breathe between dances. With a strange new dread, she saw Forrest walking toward her.

He merely put his hand on her waist. He did not even ask if she wanted to dance. She stepped quickly away from him.

"No thank you," she said.

"Come on," he replied stubbornly. "Everyone's watching. Don't embarrass me."

She smiled up at him. "Not for all the money in the world."

"Come on, then," he said again.

"No."

"Why not?" he demanded.

"Because, Forrest, I am tired. I am so tired. I'm so fucking tired of all of you. So leave me the hell alone." Shock registered on his face and for the first time, she noticed how unremarkable his perfect features were. How bland. She hoped the baby would not look like him.

Suddenly exhausted, she turned and walked away from him. She was searching through the crowd for Will and her parents when she felt a warm, strong hand on her shoulder. She turned impatiently, harsh words forming on her lips. "Leave me alone. I told you—"

Mr. Steinberg was looking down at her, amusement in his eyes.

"This is the first time I could get near you all evening," he said.

"And you're ready to bite my head off."

"Oh, I'm sorry. I didn't realize it was you." An unexpected tenderness swept through her at the sight of him.

"I was hoping we could have one dance, at least."

"At least?" she repeated, not understanding his words, only marveling at the rich timbre of his voice.

"Well," he looked slightly away, then back into her eyes. "I guess we had sort of a bad beginning. I mean, with this crazy rule about students and teachers. But I won't be a teacher here—and you won't be a student—forever."

She blushed slightly as the memory of making love to him enclosed her in a warm circle of desire, but she smiled. The music started, and he drew her to him.

There was little need to speak after that, so she rested in his arms, letting him guide her across the floor. She felt an urgent need growing deep within her, and her muscles tensed as she realized how much she wanted him.

The lights went up, and she looked at the watch on his wrist. "I have to go now," she said. "It's time to change for the supper."

"Will I see you again?" he asked quietly. "I don't care how or where. But I haven't been the same since we—well, I really need to be with you. A lot."

"Even if it means your job?" she asked, incredulous.

"Julie, I haven't been able to think of anything else, since the last time we were together." He sounded sincere. "I've had other jobs but I've never had anyone like you." He took her hand and drew her fingers to his lips. "I want to be with you. I know what you're going through, and I want to help."

"You want to help?" she repeated, smiling up at him. "You mean it?"

"I mean it. I'll marry you. Or live in sin with you. I'll help you with the baby—raise it as my own. I'll do whatever you want, whatever you need. I just want to be with you."

"All right. I—I'll see you tomorrow," she promised, stunned. He bent down to kiss her cheek just as Will came to claim her.

She felt like a dream, like Cinderella, as she pulled off her evening gown and tossed it in the corner behind her little bed. Amanda was still up studying, but Julie refused her offer to help. To Julie's relief, her mother had gone with the judge to the banquet hall. She wanted—needed—to think about this new development. Maybe she wasn't going to be a single mom after all. Maybe she was going to be Mrs. Gregory Steinberg. Her father would be appalled if she married a Jew, but she didn't care. She might even love Mr. Steinberg, if what she felt for him at that moment was love.

She was in the bathroom washing her hands when it happened. First she was just dizzy, then the pain hit her hard in the lower abdomen and simultaneously in her back. Weakly, she sank to the floor as she felt the flow of blood start; then suddenly, it was all over.

Looking at it, she felt both anguish and disbelief. Small as it was, a tiny form was distinguishable. It was no more than three of four inches long, but it had arms and legs like a regular baby, and its head was curiously masked by a milky, white substance.

She heard the door open, and Amanda asked, "Hey, what's the holdup? Will is waiting—"

"Amanda," Julie whispered hoarsely, and her voice caught in a little sob. With great effort, she regained control. "Bring me a towel and clean underwear. Please."

Amanda understood. She got the items and asked, as she handed them through the bathroom door, "Are you all right? Can I help?"

"No, I'm fine," Julie replied, pulling herself up beside the basin.

"Tell Will I'll be a few more minutes."

Amanda pushed her way inside, and if the mess on the floor bothered her in the least, she gave no indication.

"You can't go out again. You should have a doctor. At least the dorm nurse—"

"No! There's no need. I'm really okay. Just a little weak, that's all." Her teeth chattered as she spoke. She was freezing.

Amanda watched as Julie finished rolling the towel into a cylindrical bundle.

"Is that it?" she asked.

Julie nodded.

"Can't you flush it?"

"No," Julie replied emphatically: "I thought about it but . . . I just couldn't." She placed the terrycloth cylinder carefully on the floor beside the sink and started rinsing out her panties. "I'll be all right, Amanda. Really." She wished her roommate would leave so she could wash herself.

"Well, you're not going to any dinner, Julie Carson."

"Come on, I have to go. Mama and Daddy—"

"Never mind. I'll tell Will to make up some excuse. Now, if you don't get yourself right into bed, I'm going to call a doctor, and then Will and I will go for your mother. And I mean it. You could hemorrhage or something."

"I won't. Listen, do you have any change?"

"I think so."

"Could you go down the hall and get me a sanitary napkin? The bleeding's almost stopped already, but I don't think I should try to use a tampon. Okay?"

When Amanda returned, Julie had wiped up the floor and gotten into bed. The towel and its contents lay on top of the covers, near her feet.

Amanda nodded at the bundle. "What are you going to do with it?"

"In the morning, when I feel better, I'll take it out to Mama's farm and bury it out there. That's the only thing I know to do. But for now, I want it close to me, for just a little while."

"What do you want me to tell Will?" asked Amanda.

"Just that I'm tired from the dance. And ask him if he'd go by the banquet hall and apologize to my folks, and whatever he does, not to let Mama come up here. He can tell them I'll call them tomorrow." She felt drugged. "All I want right now is to sleep."

"Look, Julie. I feel responsible. If anything happens—"

"Will you stop? You're worse than my mother!" Julie smiled at her friend. "Okay. If it'll make you quit fretting, I'll go to the infirmary first thing in the morning."

"Why not now?"

"Look, it's Saturday night. There's probably no one on duty but the janitor. I probably wouldn't be able to see a doctor before morning anyway, and you know it. I just want to sleep, okay?"

Amanda shook her head. "I don't like it."

"You and Will can pick me up in the morning and take me over. Will that do?"

"Will can pick us up. I'm not leaving you alone tonight!"

"Now you're just being plain silly. What are you going to do? Watch me sleep? Please," her voice faded to a whisper, and tears welled in her eyes. "I'd sort of like to be alone, if you don't mind. And please don't tell anyone yet, not even Will."

Amanda nodded, then went to the closet for an extra blanket. "We'll be here early. You better be ready. And call me at Will's if you start to feel worse. Promise."

Julie agreed, and when Amanda spread the blanket over her, she reached up and embraced her. "Thanks," was all she said.

Suddenly, before either of them could do more than look up, the door opened and the dorm house mother came in without knocking.

"Dear, your young man is waiting so patiently," she told Julie. "I told him I'd see what's keeping you. Everyone else left long ago."

"Oh, I'm sorry, Mrs. White. I have a headache. I got my period, and I really don't feel like going to the supper. It took me by surprise, and I always get the most awful cramps."

Mrs. White winked conspiratorially, "Thank heaven for small favors, anyway," she said. "What's this? Laundry?" She picked up the towel.

"Just dirty linens. I'll take care of it in the morning."

"Nonsense. No time like the present. I'll just pop it in the chute for you. Rest well, my dear."

Julie felt sick as she watched Mrs. White tuck the bundle under her arm and head down the hall. Her eyes met Amanda's, which were full of compassion and understanding.

"It's probably for the best," Amanda tried to comfort her.

Julie nodded. "I'm so tired. I just want to go to sleep. Would you turn the light off on your way out?"

"Yeah. Okay, then. Goodnight."

"Goodnight," Julie replied drowsily.

The door clicked softly shut behind her roommate. Julie shifted her position under the blankets, trying to find relief from the dull pain at the base of her spine. Finally, she got Amanda's pillow from the other bed to place under her back.

The moonlight spilled across her hair and face as she burrowed deeper under the covers. She tried not to think of the loss, only of what she had gained. Maybe the knowledge of what life was really all about would prove to be worth the cost. She thought of Gregory Steinberg and was comforted. She could never go back now to the superficial, empty life her family and society had always arranged for her comfort and convenience.

It was going to be all right. There would be other babies. Greg Steinberg's babies—little cousins for the babies Amanda would have with Will. Life would go on, and now she would be a full participant, not just a frilly decoration.

She couldn't stop shaking, she was so cold. Shivering, she pulled the blankets closer around her. Everything would be fine. She would sleep, and the morning would greet her bright and shining and full of love. Everything would be all right, if only she could get warm again.

Chapter Eighteen

Amanda stirred slowly, reluctantly, into wakefulness. Then, gradually becoming aware of the long, lean form next to her, she opened her eyes. For a few minutes, she watched him sleep. Will was even more handsome than she'd first thought, now that he'd shaved off his beard. He had one arm thrown back over his head and his full lips parted as his chest moved noiselessly, slowly, up and down. His legs were stretched straight out in front of him, and his feet extended slightly beyond the end of the mattress. Beneath the sheet, the muscles of his thighs stood out firm and strong. Again, she felt the ever increasing, almost overpowering need of him.

If only, she thought as she watched him, there was some kind guarantee in life. She would be willing to bargain for the proverbial happy ending. If she could be sure that for the next few years she could wake up beside him, she would gladly agree to shorten her life. What an egotist God must think her, to presume her life would be worth such bliss. She laughed.

"You keep doing that," he warned, his eyes still closed. "And it could get to be a habit."

A gentle rain was falling outside, and peals of thunder sounded in the distance. With quiet determination, he pulled her to him; and his hands swept possessively over her body, resting just long enough on each susceptible area he now knew so well. As always, when she lay with him, she was mute at first, almost paralyzed with the ecstasy of feeling him against her. And slowly, as always, she responded to his every touch until at last she begged him to take her.

When finally he did, her eyes opened wide with the first shock of his force. Still inside her, he now gazed down at her, his passion showing in a tender smile. The usual feeling of helplessness swept over her, and she found it difficult to breathe.

"I love you," she whispered.

"I love you, too . . . as if you didn't know."

And then he began to move again, and she moved with him; and he continued to stare into her eyes until she came again . . . and again.

Curled against each other, they slept; and when she next opened her eyes, the rain had stopped and the sun beat warm and strong through the window. The space on the bed beside her was empty. She sat up with a start.

"How do you like your eggs?" Will asked. She looked around to see him standing in the doorway.

'What time is it?" she replied as she pulled on her jeans.

"Time decent people were out of bed and doing something worthwhile. The devil makes mischief for idle hands, you know."

She grinned. "I didn't notice your hands being so idle."

"Yours either," he said and laughed. She loved hearing him laugh. "Now if you don't tell me how you want your eggs, you won't get anything 'til suppertime." He reached for her, but she slipped out of his grasp.

"Wait," she said. "I have to call Julie."

The switchboard operator took forever to answer, which was not so unusual for a Sunday morning. But at last she came on the line and put the call through, letting it ring several times before she told Amanda to try back later.

"She doesn't answer," she announced to Will.

"She's probably in the shower," he said, placing two plates of bacon, eggs and buttery toast on the coffee table. "Or washing her hair or something."

"I don't think so." An ominous knot started to tie itself in the pit of Amanda's belly.

"Whatever she's doing, she'll keep until after we eat. Come on—don't let it get cold."

After breakfast, there was still no answer.

"We have to go over there," Amanda said. "She really wasn't feeling well last night, and I promised we'd take her to the infirmary this morning."

"Maybe she asked someone to take her already."

"No. She wouldn't. She didn't even want me to mention it to you until this morning."

Common sense and logic reassured her, as they drove back to the dormitory. Julie probably was in the shower, or down the hall reliving the glory of Homecoming with some of the other girls. But Amanda would feel a lot better once Julie had seen a doctor. And she would give her hell for not staying in bed as she had promised.

There were no empty parking places near the dorm, so Will let her out at the corner and told her he would meet them in the lobby as soon as he found a spot. As Amanda walked the short distance, she marveled at the perfect day. The sun was high, and for the first time in weeks, there wasn't a hint of a cloud in the sky. The pine needles and oak leaves mingled together in a damp mulch on the sidewalk might even get a chance to dry out in time for a crunchy prelude to winter.

The dormitory was practically deserted, and as quiet as a tomb as its inmates slept off the consequences of a night of revelry. Amanda silently opened the door to the room she shared with Julie.

Julie was propped up on a small mountain of pillows, looking somewhat pale, but otherwise as pretty as the night before. Her arms lay placidly at her side, and her lovely mane of hair fell around her shoulders in a thick curtain. Her eyes were half-open, as she contemplated something on the closet door.

"What's the big idea?" Amanda demanded cheerfully. "Why didn't you answer the phone? Didn't you know I'd be worried?"

The girl made no reply.

"Julie, are you all right?"

There was a sinking stillness about the room. The clock ticked, quietly complacent as it measured the seconds. Amanda approached the bed, fear clutching at her chest. Julie still did not speak or move, or look at her. Ancient recognition of the final human state worked its way into Amanda's mind, and it seemed there was no air in her lungs, no air in the room itself. She felt as though she was in a horrible dream, a nightmare in which she wanted to scream but could not remember how.

"No. Oh, no . . ." was all she could say, over and over. "No . . . no . . . no."

She knew it was pointless but she searched for Julie's pulse. The girl's hands were like chunks of priceless marble. Amanda pulled back the blankets, and almost fainted at the sight. She had never imagined the human body contained so much blood.

It was everywhere. It covered Julie from the waist down and coated the sheets. The stench of the puddle that had formed around her hips rose to Amanda's nostrils, and she thought she was going to vomit. The shock of finding her roommate like that made her stagger for a moment but she caught herself on the bureau before she could fall. With grim determination, she steadied herself.

She took several deep breaths, her eyes closed tight to shut out the scene before her. When she could bear to look again, she gently covered Julie, tucking her arms under the blankets as she did so.

She picked up the telephone and dialed three digits. There were only two rings before a familiar voice greeted her.

"Gunila? It's me. Get up here as fast as you can."

"Mandy! Hey, where've you been? I had a gig for us the other night. Top paying clientele—"

"Be quiet and listen," Amanda cut her off. "Something has happened. Get up here as fast as you can. Hurry."

She hung up the phone. While she waited for her old partner whose room was two floors down, she tidied up the room. She smoothed the covers of her own bed and then fished Julie's formal out of the corner where it had been tossed the night before. She shook it and hung it in the closet. Then she put all the tops back on Julie's jars of cleansing cream and lotions and makeup. A tap sounded on the door, and she jumped. She opened it just wide enough to admit Gunila's slender form.

"Listen," she said. "I have to find Mrs. White and call a doctor. My roommate—"

"Is she sick?" Gunila asked, peering over Amanda's shoulder.

"I'm not sure," Amanda replied. "But I think she's dead."

"What?" Gunila backed away. "I'm not having anything to do with this. Especially if she OD'd."

"Will you shut up and listen!" Amanda grabbed Gunila's arm before she could open the door. "I'll explain later, but nothing has happened that anyone had anything to do with. In the meantime, I don't want anyone else in here. Besides," her voice almost broke despite her stony control. "She deserves some privacy. Just stay with her for a few minutes, and don't let anybody in until I get back."

Gunila agreed, and Amanda closed the door behind her as silently as she had first opened it. She had no trouble finding Mrs. White in the lounge with her morning coffee. She explained that something was wrong with her roommate, and in no-nonsense terms ordered the housemother to call an ambulance. Then she went to look for Will.

When she found him waiting patiently in the lobby, she told him about the miscarriage the night before. Julie was feeling worse, she said, that's why she hadn't answered earlier. He wanted to go up, but she convinced him that it was better to go to the Carson house, awaken Julie's parents and take them straight to the hospital. She wanted someone strong with Mrs. Carson. She couldn't bring herself to tell him what she feared. And deep inside, she clung to the belief that since this was the modern, miraculous age of science, they would somehow bring Julie back.

"Thanks," she said to Gunila when she got back to the room she had shared with Julie. Mrs. White had not come up yet. "Go on back to your room and don't say anything to anybody."

"You don't have to tell me twice," Gunila said and made a hasty departure. Amanda knew Gunila didn't believe there had been no foul play; and considering the circumstances, Amanda could not blame her for wanting to get as far away as possible. She gazed in awe at Julie's perfect, flawless skin. There was no change.

Mrs. White came in then with a young intern from the campus infirmary and Amanda heard herself, as if through a long tunnel, tell the doctor how she had found Julie that morning. Since she had learned through some of her attorney type clients that the less said the better, she had the good sense not to mention the pregnancy or the events of the night before. She knew that, more often than not, many relevant facts in a lot of cases went completely overlooked. Giving unasked-for facts would serve no useful purpose, and any premature acknowledgement of the pregnancy would implicate too many people—Julie's football hero, Amanda's friend Andy, Josh and any other boy who had come within ten feet of her in the last three or four months. And none of that could help her now.

Amanda watched the ambulance attendants lift Julie, blankets and all, onto the stretcher. She walked silently, beside her roommate's still form to the elevator, and then to the open door of the ambulance. She knew by now Will and the judge and Mrs. Carson would be on their way to the hospital. She also knew she couldn't go there. She didn't belong there, with Julie's family. And there was something else she had to do.

With resolute purpose, she went back to the room and gathered up her purse and some books, unmindful of the watchful eye of the policeman stationed there. She was glad she had straightened up Julie's things.

Blocking as much as possible out of her protesting mind and thinking only of what she had to do next, she walked over to Andy's apartment. She had to know if Julie had gone back there after all. If she had gone back there and let him try the coat hanger solution. No thought had formed in Amanda's mind as to what she would do once she found out, but she had to know.

When she reached his place, a tall girl with stringy blond hair was loading some cartons into the back of a pickup truck. Amanda walked past her onto the porch and knocked.

"He's not here anymore," the girl announced. "Who are you?"

"Just a friend," Amanda replied. "Do you know where I can reach him?"

"I can give him a message when I write," the girl said pointedly. "He's gone up to Atlanta to start his internship." With firm emphasis she added, "I'm his fiancé."

"When did he leave?"

"About two weeks ago. Listen, if you're such a good friend of his, don't you think he would have said goodbye?"

"Thanks," Amanda ignored the sarcastic attack and turned to go. Julie hadn't gone to see Andy again. It had been an accident after all, a joke of nature. Amanda could not have lived with her guilt if it had been otherwise.

She could not go back to the dorm, so she went to Will's place and tried to study but it was no use. She kept the radio on, and at every newscast she jerked to attention. When there was still nothing by the middle of the afternoon, she called the hospital. When they refused to tell her anything, she called one of her friends at the police station.

"It's about the Carson girl," she explained. "They picked her up this morning. She's my roommate at the dorm, but the doctors won't tell me anything. Can you find out how she's doing?"

"Julie Carson? You didn't hear? She's dead," he told her without sympathy. "About two a.m. She apparently had an abortion or something. Anyway, she started to hemorrhage and went into shock."

On the six o'clock newscast, campus police reported that Tallahassee's finest had recovered the fetus. It was his custom, the laundry man told the television cameras, to check the bed linens and towels for misplaced wallets and jewelry so he could return any lost items to the rightful owners. When he shook out the towels, he said, he had found the tiny baby's remains, only minutes before they would have gone into the vat of boiling, soapy water.

Waves of speculation spread across the campus.

When Amanda went to supper at the sweet shop, the students were talking of nothing else. Even Steinberg, her psychology professor, was tense and drawn. He always seemed remote and disinterested in everything around him, but he, too, was pouring over a newspaper; and when someone in the booth adjoining his turned off a transistor radio as the news came on, he asked them to turn it on again.

The cast-aside fetus and Julie's death were the result of an abortion gone wrong, the newscasters announced with relish, implying that any girl who would casually toss her baby down a laundry chute deserved no better end. With every report, the story grew more sordid. Finally, Amanda walked over to Will's apartment.

He had been there. The jeans he had worn that morning were

lying in a crumpled heap next to the bed, and his closet door stood open. When she went into the kitchen, she found the note he had taped on the cover of her history book.

"Please stay," the note invited. "There's no need to go back there. I'll call you as soon as I can."

At midnight, he still had not called. She could not imagine what he must be going through with Julie's parents. She shuddered at the thought of Julie's mother, such a frail little woman, trying to cope with her grief and all the speculation. The late-night news anchor was worse than any of the others, insinuating that an insane butcher was loose on campus just waiting for the chance to abort any unsuspecting coed. City, county and campus officials were conducting a massive search, questioning anyone and everyone who had been close to Julie.

Except me, Amanda thought dully. Julie's dead, but to protect their own fine reputations, they don't even bother to look for me.

She thought of calling the newspapers and telling them exactly what had happened, but again she gave way to common sense. All of them—everyone in the kingdom of Tallahassee—had already tried and convicted Julie of unspeakable desecrations. She could not change that, no matter what she said.

She tried to sleep, but images of a baby trying to swim through choking sudsy water haunted her dreams. Not long before dawn, she turned the radio back on. As she waited for the first light of day, she made coffee.

Will still had her car, so she took a cab to the Carson house. It gave her time to think, to try and find the right words.

She went to the front door this time and pulled the old-fashioned bell cord firmly. She thought distractedly that it must be wired to a bell inside, for it made no sound. Yet seconds later, Adele opened the door:

"May I see Mrs. Carson? I'm Julie's roommate."

"I was wondering why you didn't come," Adele said matter of factly. "That sweet child put such a store by you. Miss Julie told me you were the best friend she ever had." The woman's eyes were swollen, and her dark face ashen with her grief. She moved aside so Amanda could get past her bulk. "Come on back here in the kitchen," Adele went on. "I been keeping her mama back there with me. She's too upset to talk to all these folks, but she'll want to see you."

If Amanda had known so many people would be there, she would have postponed the visit. At least a dozen young men and women about the same age as Julie sat or stood in the living room, together with a couple of middle-aged women. They were all talking quietly. In the dining room, seated around the great oak table, were the austere friends of the judge. She recognized a couple of them, and quickly turned her face away.

Adele's shoulders were slumped and her footsteps heavy on the sky-blue carpet that led to the kitchen. The feeling of death was suffocating.

Mrs. Carson sat at the table, her hands folded together on its sparkling clean surface. She had aged ten years since Amanda had met her, only a few days before. Then, her hands clasping and unclasping spasmodically, she picked at imaginary crumbs on the Formica surface. She looked up vaguely when Amanda entered. Her eyes held the dark look of incomprehensible pain.

"Mrs. Carson, I hope you don't mind—"

"Will's at the funeral home," Julie's mother interrupted Amanda, and her voice shook slightly. "I don't know what we'd have done without him. They'll have her ready at three. Would you like to go and see her?"

"Thanks, but no," Amanda replied quietly. "I don't want to see her that way." No need to remind Mrs. Carson she had found Julie in the first place—or that she could not look more beautiful, no matter what they did to her, than Amanda would always remember her.

"Of course not," Mrs. Carson responded simply.

"It's not true," Amanda began, and faltered. She was afraid she could not go on. The constrained atmosphere was almost too much for her. "It's not true," she repeated, determined to say what she came to say. "It's not true what they're saying about Julie."

"What?" The light crept slowly back into Mrs. Carson's eyes. "Did you know about this—that Julie was—you know?" she asked in awe.

"Pregnant? Yes," Amanda said, and plunged ahead. "She was very happy about the baby. She never would have done what they're saying. She was going to tell you as soon as Homecoming was over."

"It would mean so much to me to know," Mrs. Carson appealed to her. "Could you tell me? Tell me how all this came about. Was she—did she love the boy, at least? Did he love her?"

"Yes," Amanda lied. "She never told me who it was, but she did say they planned to be married soon. The day Julie brought me here to dinner? She was going to tell you then. But she changed her mind. You see, she felt the baby move that day, for the first time. So she decided to give you Homecoming. She said that after all you've done for her, it was the least she could do for you. She didn't want you to worry."

"Oh," Mrs. Carson said faintly, and her voice gave way as tumultuous sobs wracked her slight frame. Adele cradled Julie's mother in her arms as if she were a small child. The black woman looked up at Amanda.

"She hasn't cried until now," she said. "She needed to cry."

Amanda nodded and turned to go, and she found herself standing face to face with the judge. His complexion was flushed, and his shoulders slouched beneath the sorrow they carried. But his eyes, though ringed with the shadows of a sleepless night, held her in undisguised contempt. He recognized her now, no question about it. She wondered, as if it mattered, exactly when he had realized who she was. The mayor stood at the judge's side, perspiring nervously. Will's broad form loomed behind them.

"Get out of my house," Judge Carson told her through clenched teeth.

"Now, there's no need to go upsetting yourself," the mayor admonished, trying to calm him. "I'm sure, now that Mandy has offered her condolences, she'll be going on back to the campus. Right, Mandy? You certainly don't intend to stay?"

Amanda looked incredulously from one to the other. She couldn't believe it. What was wrong with them? Didn't they know that who she was, and what she'd done in life—just to try and survive—had little significance in light of what had happened? Julie was dead. She wasn't coming back, ever.

She intended to go past them without even acknowledging them and let herself out the front door. She had done what she needed to do, and there was nothing more to say. Will remained in the doorway of the kitchen, blocking her exit.

"Come on," he said quietly. "I'll drive you back."

"You'll do no such thing, William," commanded the judge. "I'll have a word with you before you go anywhere with this . . . woman."

"I think it can wait," Will replied as he stared straight into the older man's eyes.

"No," Amanda said, knowing what the judge intended to say to Will, and realizing it could not be put off any longer. "Stay. You're needed here. You can keep the car as long as you want."

"Wait out front, then," he said. "I'll call a cab for you. Go back to my place and wait for me. I'll get home as soon as I can."

She knew she should feel a terrible dread, but an odd sensation of relief surged through her. When the judge was finished with Will, it would be over. He would not want to even look at her, let alone touch her. But it didn't seem to matter anymore. It would, of course, when the first shock of Julie's absence subsided. Now, however, nothing seemed as bad as Julie's needless death.

The minutes passed as she sat in stunned silence beneath a large oak tree at the edge of the vast lawn. When she checked her watch, she was surprised to see that twenty minutes had passed. Still the taxi did not come. There was no way she could bring herself to go back in the house to call again. She decided to walk.

She hadn't gone the distance of a block when her little Volkswagen pulled up beside her. The door opened and Will leaned over, holding his hand out to her. She took it and got into the car. She searched his face, a silent question in her eyes and he squeezed the hand he still held.

"You'll have to bear with them for now," he said. "They hardly know what they're saying. I'm sure you understand." She nodded, and he went on, "I'm leaving next week, after my orals . . . and the funeral. This is probably the wrong time to ask you, but I want you to come with me. I know you want to go for your master's at some point, but they have colleges out west, you know. And we could be together. I have to go because I have a job waiting. And I can't go without you, so you've got to come with me. Will you at least think about it?"

She pressed her cheek against his arm. "Thank you," she said. "Of course, I'll go with you. I don't have to think about it." She couldn't stay in this place, in this time, with these people; and she would go with Will to hell if he asked her.

"It's a long trip," he went on. "But we have a lot to talk about during the drive. You can tell me all about Amanda Carey—but not all the things you've done you wish you hadn't. I don't care about any of that. I want you to tell me who you are and who you want to be. You never have, you know."

“Yes,” she whispered gratefully. “Yes, I can do that. Because now I know.”

Chapter Nineteen

Steinberg strapped the last suitcase into the luggage rack on top of his little red MG, then he took the stack of newspapers off the passenger seat and crammed them into the wastebasket that stood inside the door of his apartment. After carefully locking the door, he put the keys under the big flowerpot out by the mailbox, as his landlady had instructed.

According to the *Democrat,* Tallahassee hadn't seen such a magnificent funeral since some big political figure had died in the late 1930s. Everybody who was anybody was at Julie's funeral, from the governor and his wife right down to the chief of police.

Steinberg knew his father would probably have an ulcer attack when he heard his ne'er-do-well son had taken off again without getting his doctorate. But Greg had to get away. For once in his life, he had gotten close enough to something he really wanted, someone to whom he could have surrendered his heart. And then she was gone, just like that.

He drove fast, scarcely stopping for the lights. He didn't know where he was going but he figured he'd drive south until he couldn't drive anymore, maybe all the way down to Miami or the Keys; and then he'd call his father for the money he would need to get set up again. He had the radio blaring the loudest, most acid rock he could find. Somehow, he would shut it all out. Somehow.

Tom put the check for forty dollars in the inside pocket of his jacket so it wouldn't get wet if it started to rain again. He threw the letter away without reading it. His mother always said the same things in her letters anyway. He smiled.

With his allowance and his new part-time job at the campus bookstore, he could afford to supply his own grass, not to mention money for dates. He would not be obligated to Jason anymore. He checked his watch and saw he had enough time to visit his chick before time to go to work.

His chick. She wasn't exactly his, but they'd had a sort of silent agreement ever since the evening of the Homecoming game. She had taken the only empty seat in the crowded sweet shop. It was the seat across the table from him.

"You don't mind, I hope?" she had asked, and just like that she had started talking to him. Of course, it probably made a difference that he wasn't self conscious or shy anymore. But he didn't even have to make an effort. When she finished her dinner, she invited him over to her place for coffee.

"We have a small commune," she said. "Four of us rented a house. I have my own bedroom," she added pointedly. And later, when he had finished with her, doing to her all the things he'd learned from the prostitute, she hadn't wanted to let him go back to his dorm.

She wasn't really his type. Always talking about women's liberation and male chauvinism and her right to be anything she wanted to be. He listened patiently, too savvy to let her know he didn't agree with most of what she said. But she seemed eager for him, so she would do for now. He might even consider moving in with her—to save money—if she asked, and he had a feeling she would because she wanted sex constantly. Morning, noon, and night. He grinned.

That was fine with him.

The little red sports car turned the corner at top speed, and Tom dodged the jet of water it sprayed at him. He admired the car so much, and the driver's skill, that he didn't really mind the near miss.

"Someday," he mused aloud, thinking of all the women in the world he still wanted—intended—to sample. "That's the kind of car I'm going to have. And then they won't stand a chance. None of 'em."

He pulled the collar of his jacket up protectively as the sky darkened, and a light Tallahassee rain began to fall.

The End

Please enjoy other books by Charlene Keel, from Red Sky Presents:

The Congressman's Wife
Dark Territory
Ghost Crown
Shadow Train
Grinder's Corner
The Lodestone
Lost Treasures of the Heart
Seventh Dawn of Destiny
The Sky's The Limit

Order from Amazon.com, redskypresents.com
or your local bookstore

Special Bonus!

An excerpt from The Lodestone, Charlene Keel's historical romance

THE LODESTONE

Spring, 1828,
Countryside in central England,
North of Oakham

As Drake untied his horse and led him away from the stream and through the thick copse of trees at its edge, he heard a sound like rolling thunder. A rider galloped past him on the lane, and his horse whinnied in protest as a cloud of dust kicked up around them. An oath escaped Drake's lips as the grime of the road clung to him once again. Who the devil would ride a horse at such breakneck speed, and why?

In the distance quickly increasing between himself and the reckless rider, he could see voluminous skirts billowing around shapely ankles and small, bare feet. Her bonnet flew off, as if released by a catapult, and a cascade of copper-colored curls tumbled down. Glinting in the sun like rubies, they bounced against shapely shoulders.

A woman! The thought filled him with anticipation. And she sits a horse as well as a man! But what in blazes was she running away from? He stepped into the lane and picked up the straw hat with the blue satin ribbons that had fallen, unnoticed by its owner. As if in answer to his unspoken question, a tradesman's cart moved complacently into view. Its driver touched his forelock with a nod to Drake.

"By yer leave, sir," the ancient groom spoke respectfully. "I'll return the miss's bonnet to her." He held out a gnarled, callused hand.

Still holding the bonnet, Drake mounted his chestnut stallion.

"You'll never catch up to her at that pace, old man," he said with a grin and urged his horse forward.

The old man's voice rang out behind him like a challenge. "All due respect, sir! Ye'll not be catching up to her, either!"

Drake Stoneham was a man who did not like to be challenged, because once the challenge had been set, it must be won. His pulse quickened as he dug his heels into Prince Talleyrand's sides, then leaned forward to speak into his horse's ear, coaxing the stallion onward.

He could scarcely believe his eyes, for his mount was fast and came of pure bloodlines. Drake had been urged more than once to race him, but his interests lay elsewhere. Besides, a strong, fast horse was essential to him in his travels. Much to his chagrin, he could come no closer than two full lengths behind the girl before she pulled away as if propelled by the wind itself. He caught up with her as she rode into the expansive yard of an imposing manor house, reined in her horse, and slid gracefully from his back. Taking no heed of the footmen who came to assist her, she ran toward the rear of the house, her bare feet kicking up puffs of dust.

"What a horse," Drake murmured, smiling with appreciation while the back of his mind whispered, What a woman! Who was so careless, he wondered, to allow such a beauty to gallop about the countryside with no thought to her safety or reputation.

As he came around the side of the house, Drake had to pull up short to keep from riding over the girl. She stood firm, her hands on trim but well-formed hips, and confronted the head groom who had stepped in front of her, blocking her way to the stables.

"Tell your master William Desmond's granddaughter has come for the mare," she said in a tone that would indulge no nonsense.

"Aye, Miss Cleome. She's here," the groom responded with a jerk of his thumb to indicate the stables behind him. "Lucky for her we got to 'em in time. If Major Domo had mated her again, she would have been done for, she would."

"Not while there's breath in my body!" the lovely Cleome declared, and Drake smiled, enjoying the sight of a pretty lass so ready to do battle for her horse. As the side door of the elegant mansion flew open, she spun around to face a gentleman of at least threescore and five. He stormed across the marble patio and into the yard, heading straight for the startled girl. Drake could tell by the set of his mouth and crimson blaze of his complexion that he was furious. Cleome's groom and his pony cart were nowhere to be seen, so Drake quickly dismounted. It appeared the enchanting equestrienne would be in need of assistance, which he would be happy to give.

"It will not be necessary to tell the master anything," the old gentleman said gruffly. "For he is standing here before you."

She froze, her face blanched as white as the king's new linen. But then she took a deep breath and walked over to the gentleman with what Drake considered an admirable display of courage for one so small, and a woman besides.

"I have come for my horse," she said stoutly.

"I've warned William Desmond repeatedly about that mare," the man informed her in a pompous, nasal voice. "If it happens again, I swear I shall teach her with my own whip to mind her manners."

"But Lord Easton," Cleome reasoned. "Your groom has told me no harm was done. And even so, we are quite prepared to care for any result, as we did the last time."

"My dear young woman," his lordship snapped. "I would prefer Major Domo save his—" here he paused a moment in deference to Cleome's delicate sex. "Ah—save his strength for a thoroughbred."

Color flooded Cleome's face and anger flashed in her blue eyes. She replied quietly, "Please believe, milord, I would prefer the same for my mare!"

It was all the footmen and groom could do to contain their mirth at such effrontery but stifle it they did. Lord Easton's eyebrows shot up in surprise that this slip of a girl would address him with such disrespect—and hurl such an insult upon his horse. He spluttered in vexation, at a complete loss for words.

Drake leaned against his horse, thoroughly enjoying the entertainment. The young beauty didn't seem to need his aid after all. Deep, baritone laughter rang out behind Lord Easton and the girl, and a handsome youth stepped into the yard, grinning broadly. He was dressed in an elaborate riding costume, and he cut a fine figure with his thin frame and his golden curls. He seemed quite as amused by the situation as Drake was.

"I say, Father," he quipped brightly, aiming every ounce of his charm at Cleome. "It hardly seems honorable to whip a lady merely for following the dictates of nature—and there was no rendezvous after all." Cleome bristled at his words, but he stepped up to her and caught her hand. "What? Not even a hello for me, after all these years? Why, Cleome . . . such manners!"

"Hello, Garnett."

"Enchante," he murmured, bending to brush her hand with his lips. With no apology, she pulled it away from him.

"Get the damned horse!" Lord Easton barked at his groom. As the servant rushed to do his bidding, he warned Cleome anew, "I promise you, impertinent miss, if she finds her way here again, it will be the last time."

Cleome led Molly to the edge of the lawn where the old man Drake had passed on the road was pulling the Shetland to a halt. She quickly tied the mare to the back of the cart, then she went to the splendid colt that had conveyed her to the Easton estate. With a slight bow, Drake held her bonnet out to her as she passed him.

"I believe this is yours, mademoiselle," he said.

With a terrible shock, Cleome realized a stranger had witnessed the entire uproar. Her grandmother, if she were still alive, would have severely chastised her for acting "like lowborn Liverpool trash." A blush crept into Cleome's cheeks and heightened them to a warm glow as she looked up into smoky, hazel eyes fringed with dark, thick lashes and sparkling with unspent laughter.

"Thank you, sir," she said as she took the bonnet from the tall stranger. She turned away from him and hastily replaced it, trying to restore her hair to some semblance of order. By the time she had tied the ribbons, this giant of a man was bending in front of her beside Epitome, his hands forming a stirrup; and she realized she had also lost her slippers somewhere along the way. Her blush deepened but she allowed him to help her onto Epitome's back. His warm flesh cupping the naked arch of her foot inspired within her a mysterious longing such as she'd never experienced.

She nodded with as much dignity as possible to the small company of gentlemen, then motioned for Old Sam to follow her. He touched his brow to Lord Easton, the younger Easton, and the stranger, then he dutifully followed his mistress down the lane and into the forest, going back to the Eagle's Head the way they had come.

"She has grown into a real beauty, has she not?" Garnett said, looking after Cleome with undisguised longing.

"That piece of baggage is none of your business, sir," Lord Easton informed him curtly. "I will thank you to remember your place and allow her to keep to hers."

"Daresay, you do not take her grandfather's place into consideration when there's cribbage or whist going on ever there," the young man retorted pleasantly.

"Yes . . . well. All men are equal on the turf, and under it! Indeed, in any game of chance if a man's purse is sufficient to his daring. What you have in mind for that lass is considerably different, I wager."